AN INVITATION TO BE PART OF PEPPER'S LITTLES LEAGUE!

Want to read more stories featuring Littles? Join Pepper North's newsletter. Every other issue will include a short story as well as other fun features! She promises not to overwhelm your mailbox and you can unsubscribe at any time.

As a special bonus, Pepper will send you a free collection of three short stories to get you started on all the Littles' fun activities!

Here's the link:

http://BookHip.com/FJBPQV

DADDY'S WATCHING

PEPPER NORTH

Photography by TONYA CLARK PHOTOGRAPHY
Cover Model TRAVIS NORWOOD
Edited by CHERYL'S LITERARY CORNER

Text copyright© 2021 Pepper North
All Rights Reserved

CHAPTER 1

"Let me know when you have those reports, Elaine," Easton Edgewater requested from the door to her office.

"Will do. I'll get them to you as soon as possible. I know there's a lot riding on how the numbers look this quarter," Elaine answered her boss as her fingers tightened on the folders in her hands.

"Take the time that you need for accuracy. I know these reports are a bear to complete, but you're right. Speed is important. I appreciate your efforts, Elaine. I couldn't ask for a better second-in-command."

Elaine nodded and turned into her office. It wasn't as elaborate as the CEO's, of course, but it was spacious and welcoming. She passed the empty desk with the cleared wooden surface with a grimace. *Damn, I need an assistant.* Once in her private space, she dropped the folders on the cluttered desktop and collapsed into her chair.

She gave herself exactly ninety seconds to whine inside at having to complete the reports. They were her least favorite thing to do. *I love seeing it all laid out for the company when it's finished.*

With that cheerier thought in mind, Elaine turned on her computer and got started. She was deep into the first set of data when an air horn bleated incredibly close.

Reacting instinctively, Elaine jumped from her chair. Standing next to her desk, she attempted to control her racing heartbeat for several seconds before dashing into the adjourning room. A handsome young man looked up from her assistant's desk with a grin.

"Sorry. I bet that interrupted your train of thought. I'll put it in the bottom drawer," he apologized.

"Who are you?" she asked, staring at the devastatingly charming man, filling the chair so attractively. With ruffled black hair and eyes so dark she could sense their color even from a distance, he presented such a picture that she had to school her expression into stern disapproval instead of drooling. That wouldn't do.

"I'm Fane—your new assistant. Sharon picked me out of the admin pool to come replace your old one. You go through a lot," he shared as he pushed up the black-rimmed glasses that did nothing to disguise his good looks.

That assessment stopped her from sightseeing. She stared at him, unable to answer his insinuation that she was tough to work with. Good assistants were hard to find. *I'll hold on to one as soon as I find the right fit. It's not my fault that I expect the highest level of competence and dedication.*

This man would have been her absolute last choice. Laughter lines bracketed his mouth and his brown eyes twinkled. With finger-tousled hair and cuffs rolled up to reveal elaborately tattooed forearms, there was no way he fit the professional profile she needed to greet visitors to her office, even in the black horn-rimmed glasses that partially cloaked his obvious wild side.

Trying to pull her eyes away from the charismatic man, she noticed the large box sitting on the desk. A variety of brightly colored items spilled over the top: a Frisbee, a large tie-dye colored stuffed bear, a plastic golf club, a wooden handle... that wasn't a... Elaine looked at him in disbelief.

"I don't think this will work, Fane..." Elaine began, trying to be diplomatic.

"Sharon told me not to let you scare me off. She thought you needed something different." He stood to spread his arms, drawing her attention to his toned body. "You got me."

Closing her mouth with a snap, Elaine pivoted and stalked forward into her office, slamming the door behind her. *We'll just see about that!*

She picked up the phone and called Sharon's cellphone. It connected, and she heard the former executive assistant say as if she were a recording: "Welcome to Edgewater Industries, you've reached the Administrative Assistants Pool. We have restricted your privileges due to system overuse. Fane Bogart is your permanent assistant, with Easton Edgewater's approval. Have a good day."

"Sharon! Stop this nonsense. I can't work with this man... he brought *toys* to the office."

A click answered her statements as the phone disconnected.

"What?" Elaine looked at her phone in astonishment. Sharon had just hung up on her. "Enough!"

She'd handle this. Elaine walked into the outer office, ignoring her new assistant's cheerful welcome back as he decorated the top of his desk with a large blue stuffed bunny. Stomping out the door in determination, Elaine headed for Easton's office.

"I need to see Easton!" she barked on her way to the door. After attempting to twist the handle, Elaine turned to look at her boss's new secretary. "This is urgent."

"Mr. Edgewater left this note with me," Piper shared, lifting a small sticky note.

"Deal with it?" Elaine read incredulously.

"I know we don't know each other well yet, Elaine. I have gotten to know a lot of the other administrative assistants. He's the one everyone goes to when they need help with a problem. Everyone thinks the world of him. Give Fane a chance. There are several divisions that would leap at the chance to get him assigned for their group."

"They can have him. Fill me in on Easton's schedule. What's his first opening?"

Elaine watched Piper pull up a schedule on the computer. When

Piper announced a date two months in advance, she stared at Piper in disbelief. "That can't be his first available appointment."

"Mr. Edgewater blocked out a freeze on changing employee assignments until that day. You can have the first time at eight," Piper offered cheerfully.

"This is ridiculous." Elaine turned on one high heel and returned to her office.

"How can I help you with the report?" Fane asked as she entered.

"Stay out of my office and be quiet," she hissed before closing the door. Elaine heard his response before it clicked.

"I'm here when you need me."

"Never!" Elaine swore under her breath.

* * *

Two hours later, she couldn't put it off any longer. Elaine had to use the bathroom. Standing, she paused to roll her head in a circle and wiggle her shoulders back into place. Tension from looking at all those numbers and stacks of data had given her a stress headache. Well, that and missing lunch.

She walked briskly to the door and paused with her hand on the knob. When she leaned in to press her ear to the wood, Elaine caught herself. No one would make her hide in her office! Flinging open the door, she strode through the outer office, rubbing her temple to try to ease the pain away.

"Good afternoon. I brought…"

Fane's words died out as she continued down the hall to the women's restroom. That would show him. She'd just ignore him.

Quickly using the restroom, Elaine washed her hands and wet a paper towel to wipe the back of her neck in a vain attempt to revitalize herself. She frowned at her reflection. Pale and drawn, Elaine looked just like she felt—overworked and stressed out.

Slower this time, she traveled through the hallway to her office. Pausing outside the door, she gathered her professional persona and walked into the office. Fane came out of her office with a smile.

"I just..."

"Don't go into my office. There is classified information on my desk," she snapped.

"I understand, Elaine. I didn't mess..."

"Good. Just leave me alone," she cut him off as she walked through the door and closed it firmly. Resting her forehead against the panel, Elaine despaired. She'd never make it two months this angry at the incompetent man.

Turning to head to her desk, Elaine stopped in her tracks. Sitting on the desk was an iced coffee, a sandwich, two painkillers, and the stuffed blue bunny. She walked slowly forward to sink into her chair. Picking up the tablets first, she swallowed them with a sip of the drink. Elaine clapped her hand over her mouth to muffle the moan of delight at the delicious taste—exactly how she liked it.

Without thinking, she picked up the stuffie and hugged it. It was absolutely squishable and soft. Looking at the closed door, she felt bad. She wasn't giving him a chance. Fane had obviously gathered information about her favorite drink and had ordered lunch for her. In one half day, he had taken more interest in her than any of her previous administrative assistants.

At a light knock on her door, Elaine said softly, "Thank you."

"Need anything else?" he asked through the wooden barrier.

"No, this is great."

"Good."

She waited for him to say anything else, but Fane didn't. A few seconds later, she set the stuffie aside and picked up a sandwich half—turkey on wheat with mustard and sweet pickles. Her favorite. Taking a big bite, Elaine chewed in enjoyment. Within a few minutes, she tossed the wrapper in the trash. She'd been starving.

Elaine picked up her drink and took a long sip as she considered the door. If he kept the air horn and that embarrassing paddle put away, maybe she could deal with him. She decided to use the two months as a trial period. Pulling up her email, she sent Fane a message.

. . .

While I'm concentrating on these reports, I need you to set up two-hour meetings with the heads of each division beginning next month. Do not schedule more than one a day. The topic will be future expansion plans. They are to prepare a report of their current staffing and what they would need to handle a double workload. Thank you.

With that completed, she turned back to the report she was compiling. After a couple of late nights, Elaine knew she'd be able to wrap it up. Losing herself in the data, she clicked through the next bit of needed information.

CHAPTER 2

At seven o'clock, Elaine logged out of her computer as she noisily sucked the last drops of liquid from the melted ice in the plastic cup. Her mind was done. She had reached the point where she couldn't concentrate.

Reaching down, she tucked Blueberry into her desk drawer. She wanted to take her back to her apartment but didn't want to be seen carrying the stuffie. She'd have to remember to bring a tote bag.

Elaine forced her swollen feet back into her shoes and stood with a groan. Thank goodness she only had a short distance to make it to her apartment in the B tower. She knew most of the employees that chose to stay there were Littles who wished to live in the security and community of the Edgewater apartment building instead of alone in a house. Easton cared about all his employees but had a soft spot for the Littles. Elaine was sure she wasn't the only non-Little in the tower. That would be weird.

She pushed that thought from her mind. Dropping the empty cup into the trash with regret, Elaine grabbed her purse and walked to the office door. Fane's deserted desk was now decorated with a variety of fun figurines and toys. With a quick look toward the hall to make sure no one was watching, she leaned over to examine a few more closely.

"You can pick them up if you'd like," a deep voice commented behind her.

"Eek!" Elaine twirled around, suddenly energized by the thought of the picture she presented with her derriere pointed directly toward the door. "I thought you'd left for the day."

"Nope. Not until you head home. What if you'd needed me to do something? When you finish the report, we'll take off a few hours early to do something fun."

"I don't do that. I always work late," Elaine crisply stated.

"Then you need more fun in your life, away from work. Mr. Edgewater wouldn't want you to burn out," he stated with confidence as he circled around to herd her toward the door. "I've got the department meetings scheduled and on your calendar. We'll go over everything tomorrow to make sure it works well for you."

"You got everything scheduled?" she asked, searching his face for deceit.

"Of course. I know all the admins at the top of each division. We all work well together. Now, it's time for you to go home and relax. You live in B Tower, right?" Fane probed.

Mentally exhausted, Elaine started to nod but caught herself. She shouldn't tell him where she lived. "I don't think that's any of your business."

"I'm glad you're being safe. Remember, I don't know your floor or your apartment number. I just happened to see you heading into that tower one evening after I worked out."

"Oh!" she said, nodding her understanding of the circumstances as she relaxed once again.

"Besides, Knox's team wouldn't let me upstairs without being with you or having my name at the front desk. I'm just going to walk you to the tower to make sure you get there."

"Oh!" she repeated before adding, "You don't have to do that. It's safe here on the Edgewater grounds."

"I know." Fane gestured for her to precede him out of the office.

They walked silently to the elevator through the abandoned hallways. When he stepped in front of her to press the down button, his sculpted form only passably cloaked under the professional clothing drew Elaine's gaze. Immediately, when she realized what she was doing, Elaine forced herself to look away from his body. It wouldn't do for her to be ogling her assistant. She looked around to make sure no one was watching and sighed in relief to find them alone.

"You work too hard," Fane commented upon hearing the slight sound.

"I have a demanding job," she countered curtly.

"You do an amazing job. Edgewater Industries is lucky to have you. The company needs you to be able to do your job. Working through the evening every night will burn you out quickly."

"You don't need to worry about that," she reminded him of their status.

"I do and I will," he answered, looking honestly concerned.

"Here we are," she announced, stepping out of the elevator on the ground floor.

"You don't need to walk with me," Elaine assured him as they emerged into the warm evening air. She looked at him when Fane fell into step with her on the sidewalk leading toward her apartment. "Really."

"My parents taught me better than leaving someone to walk by themselves at night. Besides, I need to walk away the stiffness from sitting too long."

Silence stretched between them as she tried to come up with something to say. Peeking up at the tall man, Elaine couldn't observe any discomfort in his expression. Fane seemed perfectly at ease with walking next to her without talking. She tried to relax.

Finally, she couldn't stand it. "Can you say something?"

"Of course. What would you like to talk about? How about what we're going to do when you finish this report?" he suggested.

"We're going to do something together when I finish the quarterly reports?" she asked in confusion.

"Of course. I think we should go fly a kite. It's the perfect time of year to be out in the crisp air. I have a phenomenal one. It's incredible up in the air but takes two people to fly it. You can help me."

"What? I don't have time to go fly a kite," Elaine protested.

"You need to take some time to have fun. I need a kite-flying assistant. We both have extra time off from working for too long. Everything works out perfectly for us to do that together." He wrapped up the suggestion in a tidy packet.

"You and I aren't friends. You work for me." Elaine felt like she needed to point out their dynamic again.

"Think of this as team building. We have to learn how to work together. Here's your building," Fane pointed out, opening the front door for her. "Are you allergic to anything?"

"That's a weird question," she answered, looking at him skeptically.

"Maybe. I collect random bits of information. So, are you?"

"No. Well, something that blossoms in the spring makes me sneeze."

"Good to know. I hate the color green."

"Even more random?" she questioned and then preceded him into the lobby.

"Hi, Knox!" he greeted the large security man at the desk.

"Hey, Fane." Knox's serious tone didn't change at all as he addressed Elaine. "You're working too hard."

"Enough, you two. The quarterly reports take time," Elaine rebuked them as she walked through the lobby toward the elevator. Pressing the button, she tried to ignore their conversation.

"You're working for Elaine, now?" Knox's gravelly voice probed.

"Yep."

She listened intently to hear if he added anything else about how he felt about the new position. Fane, however, didn't elaborate.

"I bet you'll be good for each other," the security man observed before changing the topic. "You're not headed for the gym, are you?"

"Definitely. Want to come spot me on the weights?"

"I haven't gotten there yet today. I'll meet you there in fifteen or as soon as my replacement can get here," Knox agreed.

Elaine stepped into the elevator. As the doors closed, she heard the front door close behind Fane, and Knox on the phone, asking someone for a replacement at the front desk. She leaned against the elevator wall. What had happened today? It seemed like everything had changed in the last thirteen hours.

In her apartment, she dropped her clothes into the pile to go to the dry cleaners. Walking in her underwear to the bathroom, she looked at the large tub longingly before dismissing that idea after a glance at the clock. She needed to get to bed.

Elaine tried not to notice the small basket of bath toys at the bottom of the closet as she grabbed a fresh towel. It had been too long since she'd had the luxury of sitting in warm water for an extended time.

"Soon!" she promised herself aloud as she closed the door with a firm click.

Tossing the towel over the shower rod, Elaine turned on the water and stepped inside. She was careful to not get her hair wet as she washed herself quickly. Thankfully, her hairstyle was simple and matched with her need to wash it only a couple of times a week. Tomorrow would be soon enough.

Within minutes, she climbed into her bed and turned off the light. Pulling her stuffed roly poly from under her pillow, she hugged the cuddly gray bug to her chest. "Ballsy, you won't believe what happened today. I'll tell you tomorrow when we wake up if that's okay?"

When all his feet waved their approval, Elaine hugged her long-time stuffie tight and closed her eyes. "Night, Ballsy."

CHAPTER 3

Walking into her office the next morning, Elaine looked immediately at her admin's desk. Her conversation with Ballsy had highlighted how well Fane had taken care of her yesterday. The stuffie had been impressed and eager for her to get to work to see what today would bring with the fascinating man. Reclassifying her disappointment to see it empty, she funneled her emotion into anger that he was shirking his job.

"He can't even get here on time?" she fumed aloud.

"Five minutes early with coffee," a cheerful voice reassured her from the door.

When she whirled around, Fane greeted her, "Morning, boss. Did you sleep well last night?"

"Y... Yes," she sputtered with surprise. "Good morning."

"Here's your coffee, just as you like it." He handed her a large cup of the icy mixture.

"How do you know how I take my coffee?" she asked as she took the cup. "Mmm! That's better than normal," Elaine commented.

"Boss Management 101," he announced as if that were an actual class somewhere. "It's always essential to know the most important details about the person you're working with."

"Hmm… That's probably right. It is important to know the person you're working for," she commented.

"Not working for. Working with. Administrative assistant," he reminded her as he pointed to his chest.

She looked at him blankly, not understanding why he was making such a distinction between their words. Elaine knew she was the boss and he was her employee. "Whatever. Let's go over the schedule you made. Maybe you didn't get all the departments…"

"Eleven key departments, categorized by importance to the expansion plans that Easton Edgewater is investigating," Fane interrupted her to complete her statement. "Would you like to sit at my desk? Or shall we use yours to spread out the schedule I organized?"

Before she could answer, he added, "Now? Or as a break from the report you're working on?"

"Oh!" Elaine whirled to face her office door, unable to believe that she had lost track of the importance of finishing the report. "It will have to wait until later."

As she rushed to the door, her coffee sloshed icily in the plastic cup. Reminded of his thoughtfulness, she lifted it slightly toward him. "Thanks!"

"You're welcome. I'll come in later to give you a break and to go over the schedule."

"Maybe…" she commented absentmindedly as she walked into her office. Within minutes, she was absorbed in the data and unaware of him moving in the outer office.

* * *

FANE SHOOK HIS HEAD. He could see why there had been such a turnover in assistants for Elaine. His new boss wasn't deliberately mean. She worked too hard and couldn't empathize with the previous assistants who had worked with her. Elaine concentrated completely on the job at hand—not on the extraneous effects her dedication and long hours had on others.

The complaints from his fellow administrative assistants had snagged his attention first. Once he'd met Elaine, he knew that there was more to her than the superficial grievances of his colleagues. She was a complex puzzle that intrigued and attracted him—activating his Daddy protectiveness and pride as she achieved so much in the company. Even in the eyes of those who didn't want to work for her ever again, Edgewater's second-in-command was integral to the company's success.

If he read her correctly, she'd stressed her body to the breaking point and needed better nutrition and exercise. She wouldn't like his assistance at first, but somehow taking care of the maxed executive was important to him. Step one had been adding nutrition to her coffee that he suspected was her only breakfast. Lightly sweetened vanilla protein powder was the perfect answer.

Settling down at his desk, Fane created a second schedule, breaking the day into four parts. He set the timer on his watch for two hours and dove into work. Her office and online files were in atrocious shape. The rapid turnover of one admin to another had compounded the mismatched filing and organizational systems.

When the timer on his watch beeped, Fane put his computer to sleep and placed heavy items on top of each stack of papers and files he'd organized. Once he was sure nothing would fly away, he walked to her office and tapped lightly on the door.

"No."

Opening the door, Fane announced, "Save your file."

Automatically, Elaine pressed the keys on her computer. Looking up at him, she asked, "What's going on?"

"Safety drill. We need to evacuate the building."

"Crap!" Elaine closed her computer and lifted it to stow it in her case.

"In a drill, you're supposed to leave everything. It will be fine. Just a drill," he reminded her.

"Oh, okay." She followed him through the office to the hallway. People milled around at a normal pace, completing their daily tasks.

Stopping in her tracks, Elaine asked, "How come no one else is evacuating?"

"New evacuation program from the big guy. Only certain departments are notified at a time. Improves on productivity. We don't want to be the last ones out," he suggested, placing a guiding hand on her back and steering Elaine toward the door.

"Oh. I guess I understand that. We lose a lot of work time getting everyone outside." She preceded him into the elevator and pushed the ground floor button.

Three floors later, Elaine looked at him with a horrified expression. "You're never supposed to take the elevator in an emergency."

"Next time," Fane agreed.

They rode in silence the rest of the way. As the elevator settled on the bottom floor, Fane watched her face carefully. He could tell her thoughts focused on completing the reports. It wouldn't be a break if she didn't let her mind relax as well.

When the doors opened, he guided her outside. Pointing to the far side of a grassy area, he reported, "That's the gathering location."

"I can't walk across the grass in these shoes. That's ridiculous."

"Then we take them off." Fane knelt by her feet and instructed, "Put your hand on my shoulder for balance." Looking down at the ground, he smiled as her hand landed lightly on his shoulder and then moved experimentally, feeling the muscles under his dress shirt.

Moving quickly, he slipped her pumps from her feet and stood with her shoes in his hand. "The grass should be soft," he suggested, leading her onto the beautifully manicured lawn. Fane was pleased to see her toes wiggling in the grass as she strolled.

They walked quietly for several steps before he reminded her, "Breathe. Roll your head on your shoulders to dispel the tension there."

She followed his directions and stopped with a sigh. "There isn't an evacuation drill, is there?"

"Not an official one. You needed a break and some fresh air."

"I don't like being lied to," she stated stiffly, staring at him.

"Then I'll always tell you the truth," he answered with a smile. "This time, I didn't technically lie."

"You're the big guy who ordered the evacuation drill for two people?" she asked, remembering his words. Elaine eyed his broad shoulders and athletic shape.

Not answering with words, Fane smiled. He enjoyed seeing the physical attraction in her eyes before she concealed it. "Come on. Let's walk to the end of the grass and then we'll turn around and go back to work."

Fane gestured forward and nodded mentally when she stepped in the direction he had pointed. They walked quietly again to reach the area he had indicated and then turned to head back to the towering office building. He noted that her pace didn't quicken in anger.

"It's beautiful here," she commented softly. "I don't get to spend much time outside."

"We need to change that. Breaks are good for your mind and your heart. My first task was inserting breaks in your schedule."

"Why?"

"Because Edgewater Industries needs you to stay strong. And I want you to be healthy and happy," he shared, subtly pointing out that his concern about her was not just based on her importance in keeping the company progressing and profitable.

"Why do you care?" she asked softly, searching his face.

"Because," he replied cryptically.

"That's not really an answer," she protested as they reached the edge of the green space.

"That's all you get for now." Fane distracted her by waving her high heels. "How do you walk in these?"

"Practice."

Elaine reached out a hand to take one shoe. She protested as Fane crouched down to cup her ankle in preparation of putting them back on, "I can do it."

"Of course you can. But doing everything yourself is lonely and I want to help," he assured her as she automatically balanced herself with a hand on his shoulder. It pleased Fane to see that she was adjusting to feeling comfortable around him. Quickly, he slipped her shoes onto her feet and stood to extend a hand as she stepped back onto the sidewalk.

"Feel better?" he asked as they walked back through the large glass doors toward the elevators.

She was quiet for a few seconds before answering, "I do."

They stepped into the small enclosure, and Fane selected their floor. He remained quiet, allowing her to process through the extraordinary amount of information that must cycle through her mind. To his delight, she added, "Thank you," after a few seconds.

"You're very welcome."

When the doors opened, he escorted her down the hallway to the large office. Elaine flew into her office to immerse herself immediately in the report. Fane removed a chilled water bottle from the small fridge he had requisitioned from the central inventory. She'd left her door partially open, and he walked in quietly to not disturb her.

Cracking the lid open, Fane set the chilled bottle down by her elbow. She looked up from her computer and nodded absentmindedly before picking up the bottle and taking a large swig. He turned to leave the office when, once again, she immediately became lost in the data filling her screen.

Fane stopped in the doorway to look back at his new boss. She looked better. There was color in her cheeks and her shoulders had settled back into place instead of hunching up by her ears. Elaine would fight him every step of the way, but he would help her find joy in living as well as working.

CHAPTER 4

"How's it going, boss?"

Elaine looked up at the sound of Fane's voice and smiled at the handsome man standing in the doorway with his hands behind his back. "I think I'll finish the report tomorrow. It seemed to all come together today."

"Awesome. You're amazing."

Studying his face to see if Fane was joking or not, Elaine decided to give him the benefit of the doubt. He'd been right about everything else today. She stood and stretched her arms to each side.

"I hate being glued to that desk. I usually hibernate here when I have to create this report," she admitted. "I've actually gotten more done by taking breaks today. It's like it supercharged my efforts."

"It's good for your brain. Now, ready to get away from all of this?" Fane asked.

"I'm ready to put my feet up and chill for the night. A warm bowl of soup and some TV sounds very good."

"Would you like to go to yoga with me? It would help stretch out your muscles," Fane suggested with a gentle smile.

"Yoga? Guys do yoga?" Elaine blurted before feeling her cheeks heat with embarrassment at making the exercise sound like a female only sport.

"Yes. Men enjoy yoga as well."

"Sorry. Sometimes my mouth operates while my brain is still processing. I'll have to pass. I'm one of the few women in the world who doesn't own a pair of yoga pants," Elaine laughed as she leaned down to pull her purse from the lower desk drawer.

"Today is your lucky day. You get to join the world," Fane announced, pulling a small gift bag from behind his back.

"What is this?" she asked as he held it out to her.

"Look inside."

Elaine took the bag and peeked inside. Fabric filled the bottom. Tentatively, she pulled out the first item. It was a fitted shirt in a beautiful light lavender color. Throwing it over her arm, she extracted the second item and laughed.

"Yoga pants!" Shaking them out, she said, "Yoga pants for a very small woman."

"Yoga pants are supposed to be snug. They'll fit. I've got a pretty good eye for women's clothes."

Her good mood evaporated in a poof of anger. She began to shove everything back into the bag. When his hand closed over hers, she sent him a warning glance that usually had men running for cover.

"You can just go clothe all those women you've been eyeing," she answered before snatching her hand from his and finishing the task of putting everything back in the bag.

"I have four sisters and a fashionista mom," he replied.

It took a couple of seconds for his words to register. "You have four sisters and a mom," she repeated.

"All veteran shoppers who wanted someone else's opinion before buying anything. They also discovered that I have a super good memory and could remember who in the house had matching accessories. Knowing what clothes would fit on which sister helped prevent hurt feelings. I'm an excellent judge of sizes. Those are perfect for you."

As if it were a totally natural gesture, he stepped forward to take her hand. "Don't forget your purse," he reminded before taking a step toward the door.

"I'm not going to yoga, Fane. I'll feel totally out of place."

"This is a great beginner class. Purse, Elaine," he reminded her again as he took a step toward the door.

Automatically, she picked up her purse as he gently tugged her away. Elaine clutched the bag of clothing to her chest as she followed him out of the office. Fane stopped to pick up a small duffel bag on his desk before leading her to the elevator. He held her hand securely in his when a few others entered behind them, despite her attempts to pull her hand subtly away. When he selected the main floor, she leaned against the wall next to him and watched the numbers flash by on the display.

The elevator stopped twice, allowing the others to step out with pleasant comments about seeing them tomorrow. She met his gaze angrily as the elevator resumed its descent.

"Fane, it's not appropriate for you to hold my hand." Elaine jerked her hand from his. "I'm your boss. I'd like you to remember that."

"Gotcha," he answered easily, completely unrattled by her reprimand.

"Really, Fane. I appreciate all you did for me today. And you were totally right that if I took some breaks, I was able to focus better." Elaine juggled the items she held to redistribute them. *I don't really miss holding his hand.*

"I'm right about this, too. What's the worst thing that could happen?" he asked, watching her face.

"Yoga?" she asked, thrown off balance by his change of topic.

When he nodded, she continued, "I don't know... I could make a complete fool of myself. Do something awkward like have a cramp or tie myself into a knot. Maybe fall over? Am I going to know other people there?"

"I think you'll probably know just about everyone. Almost all of them live in B Tower. I bet you've seen them in the lobby or in the elevator."

"I don't think I'd be comfortable being in class with those I supervise," Elaine admitted.

She tried to remain separate from everyone. It was tough enough being the second in command of a major industry. Elaine had found through her years in business that things went smoother when she interacted with staff members on a purely professional basis.

"Been burned before, huh?" he asked with a knowing gaze.

Elaine nodded before she could stop herself. "I should have been more careful."

"You're never to blame for the misdeeds of others," he corrected softly. "I think you'll find the atmosphere different here."

The elevator doors opened, and Fane gestured for her to precede him. The main floor buzzed with people milling around at the end of the day. Happy laughter and a hum of conversation rang out between the employees as they made plans for the evening. Several people called their wishes for Elaine and Fane to have a good evening and she raised her hand carrying the clothing-stuffed gift bag to acknowledge their words.

Fane addressed virtually everyone by name and returned the wish for a pleasant night as they crossed the tiled floor. At the large glass doors, he stepped forward to open one. Stepping out of the building, Elaine took a deep breath of fresh air before turning toward her apartment.

When her assistant fell into step beside her, Elaine rushed to say, "You don't have to walk with me."

"It's my pleasure. My destination is in the same building."

"The yoga class?" she asked, glancing over at the handsome man. She tried not to notice the bluish highlights that appeared in his black hair under the overhead lights.

"Yes. You'll have to go right by the gym on your way up to your apartment."

"Oh! It's in the gym. I've been in there a couple of times." Elaine always tried to choose odd times to work out so she didn't sweat in front of others.

"You know people won't look at you any differently here if you take advantage of the amenities on the Edgewater campus," Fane suggested.

"It's different for a woman in my position," she tried to explain.

"You worked in some crappy situations before, huh?"

Elaine stopped and turned to look at him. "That's just how it is for a female in a supervisory position. It's best to be distant. Otherwise, people try to take advantage of you."

"I'm sorry. I think you'd find it's different here. Easton Edgewater doesn't allow those sorts of things to happen here. Perhaps you'll decide to try interacting more personally with the staff. They're a very supportive bunch," Fane suggested as they approached the entrance of B tower.

"Hi, Knox!" he greeted the enormous security man with a raised hand. "You coming to yoga tonight?"

"If I can find someone to cover the desk, I'll be there," Knox answered with a rare smile. "Good evening, Elaine."

"Evening, Knox. You do yoga?" The question burst from her lips before she could stop it.

Knox laughed. "Best thing I ever started. I'm not very flexible, but it helps keep me more balanced—inside my mind and out," he confessed.

Fane paused at the desk to talk, and Elaine eased away. She'd leave the obvious friends to chat. Pressing her hand against the elevator's electronic panel, she stared at the metal doors as an errant wish popped into her mind. It must be nice to be able to relax with everyone. As the doors opened, Elaine stepped inside, eager to escape.

Fane called, "Hold the elevator for me," and dashed across the lobby to dart between the closing doors she hadn't attempted to stop.

"Whoa! Just made it." He pressed his palm against the interior panel for clearance before selecting a floor above the one that Elaine had already activated.

The two rode silently together until the doors opened for her floor. Shifting away from the wall, Elaine stopped when Fane hooked a finger in the strap of her purse. She looked up at him in surprise.

"It's not too late. Come with me. I haven't steered you wrong yet," he reminded her with a devastatingly attractive smile. He didn't seem to be aware of the power he wielded.

"I'd have to change."

"There are locker rooms."

"And what if these don't fit?"

"They will. Four sisters and a mom," he reminded her.

"I'll fall over."

"The teacher is excellent. He'll never let that happen."

"Don't I need a mat or something?"

"Got extras in the yoga studio."

Elaine stared at him, speechless. She searched for another reason to skip the class and could come up with nothing. Being alone in her apartment suddenly sounded so… lonely.

"I guess I could try it," she relented.

"Good. Come on." He pushed the close doors button and leaned back with a smile.

"I'm not always going to do what you suggest," Elaine warned him.

"I have no doubt," he agreed with her as the door opened on the next floor. Fane said nothing else but simply pressed his free hand on the small of her back to guide her from the elevator into the large gym.

A few people worked out on various pieces of equipment. They all called their hellos before turning back to their exercise of choice. Fane led her to the door leading into the women's locker room.

"Go in and change. There are probably some people in there already. They'll reassure you that your clothes are perfectly appropriate. Class is in the studio, through that door. I'll have a mat set out for you near me."

"In the back of the class, please," she quickly stated. Elaine didn't want to be on display.

"Trust me."

She looked into his deep brown eyes and hesitated. He hadn't been wrong yet. "I'm not very good at doing that. You know, trusting people," she whispered softly.

"I know. That's changing." His hand rubbed softly on her back before lifting away. "I'll meet you inside."

Before she could change her mind, Elaine walked through the door into the luxurious changing room. Stacks of thick, absorbent towels filled the racks by the door, along with a wide variety of toiletries available for everyone's use. Turning a corner, she discovered three women inside.

"Ms. Rivers! Are you coming to yoga tonight?"

Elaine recognized Belinda from the tech center. The woman had impressed her frequently with her computer skills and willingness to pitch in to help. "Call me Elaine, please."

"I'd love to. Have you met Cynthia and Sarah? Cynthia works in the cafeteria and Sarah is Edgewater's new nurse practitioner."

"Nice to meet you," Sarah greeted her warmly before pulling off her scrub shirt to fold it and place it in her locker.

"Hi!" Cynthia said with a wave as she toed out of her black athletic shoes.

"Hi, ladies. I'm glad to meet you," Elaine said smoothly before looking down at the bag in her hand and taking a chance. "I'm trying on yoga clothes for the first time. Will you tell me the truth and keep me from making a fool of myself?"

"Of course!" Belinda assured her.

"You bet," Cynthia chimed in with a smile.

"Only if you'll return the favor. This is my first class here, too," Sarah added, looking a bit nervous.

"Thanks." Elaine relaxed a bit. Turning, she opened a locker and hung her purse from a hook. She pulled the clothes from the bag and set them on the bench that ran between the rows of storage cabinets.

"Ooo! Those are beautiful," Cynthia exclaimed. "You're going to look great in those."

"We'll see," Elaine answered, still skeptical. To her astonishment, a few minutes later, she stood comfortably dressed in her new clothes.

"You couldn't have chosen a better size," Sarah assured her. "And that color is so flattering."

"Now, if I don't fall over." Elaine seized on the next negative thought floating in her brain.

"That's what we all hope to avoid," Cynthia said fervently. "Two months with no incidents."

"You've been doing yoga for two months?" Elaine asked.

"No, for a couple of years. I toppled over doing half moon last time the class was working on that pose," Cynthia explained. "It's not any biggie if you do wobble. Everyone is fighting for balance."

Elaine nodded skeptically as the others picked up their mats. "I'll follow you."

"Really, you're going to love this," Belinda reassured her before leading the way out the door.

Self-conscious in the form-fitting clothing, Elaine mentally thanked Fane for choosing a top with a built-in bra. At least she felt fully covered and supported.

Inside the studio, the lighting was dim. Elaine relaxed a bit more away from the stark white lights of the gym area. She hesitated, looking around for Fane.

"Hey! It all fits!" his voice celebrated as he approached from the front of the room.

At the sight of him, Elaine tried to control her reaction and hoped with every fiber of her being that she was successful. Gone were the black-rimmed glasses, revealing his mesmerizing dark eyes completely. His chiseled face was even more handsomely attractive without the distraction of the heavy frames.

Fane was dressed in form-fitting yoga clothes as well. Unable to prevent herself from scanning his body as he approached, she devoured his powerful arms and chest. Those elaborate tattoos she'd dismissed as unprofessional became completely mesmerizing on his bare skin. Her gaze dropped lower as her body reacted instantly to his appeal.

The view kept getting better. Fane's shorts clung to the defined muscles in his thighs. She tore her eyes away from the package between them to note that his ink continued down his legs as well. An irresistible desire to trace the patterns with her fingertip, or better, her tongue, came over her. She ripped her eyes from his powerful calves to look at him in disbelief. In his dress clothes, he was obviously in shape, but she'd never dreamed...

When he reached her side, Fane leaned in slightly to whisper, "Told you so!"

When she looked at him blankly, trying to pull her thoughts together to figure out what he meant, Fane added, "I told you everything would fit."

"You did," she admitted, grasping frantically at the control needed to have a normal conversation with Fane. Unable to avoid the corners of her mouth tilting up in amusement, she knew she was smiling as his teasing words registered in her mind to remind her this devastating hunk was her fun-loving administrative assistant.

"Come on. Your mat's up here." Fane took her hand to lead Elaine to the mat at the corner of the front row. Others had already settled into a spot or were rolling out their mats.

"Where is your mat?" she asked, looking for another empty mat.

"I'm up there." Fane pointed to the mat that sat at the front of the room with a few items arranged in arms' reach.

"You're the teacher?" she squeaked.

"I promise not to make you fall over. Take a seat on your mat. We'll get started soon."

Fane ran a hand down her arm before he walked away to greet the others coming in. Elaine had to admit the picture he presented walking away was as arousing as the front view. *Maybe.*

Tearing her gaze from his toned butt, she looked around quickly before following the example of those around her and settling crosslegged on her mat. Elaine focused on her mat and tried to quiet her mind. This seemed like the place to do that.

"Hi, Ms. Rivers." The woman on the next mat leaned over slightly to greet her.

"Hi. Tammy, isn't it? You work in the pharmacy?"

"I do and you're almost right. I'm Tess. My mom liked an old movie featuring a Contessa. She hates that I go by my nickname."

Fane saved Elaine from having to apologize for bobbling her name by beginning the class. "All right, everyone. Settle in and begin to breathe. Close your eyes and allow all the worries of the day to disappear."

His low, melodic voice compelled her to follow his directions. Squeezing her eyelids shut, Elaine tried to follow his directions. Deep inhale and exhale. Quiet filled the dimly lit space, except for the audible rasping breath of some around her. Permeating the room, Elaine's flow of oxygen synced itself to the example surrounding her.

Sitting there quietly for a few moments, Elaine wondered how many people fell asleep just sitting there. A flurry of quiet movement made her open her eyes and look over her shoulder. Sharon knelt to unroll her mat next to Knox in the back row. She watched him discreetly help straighten Sharon's mat before patting her knee when the CEO's former executive assistant took a seat on the padding.

Fane moved to stand next to Elaine, drawing her attention, and she remembered she was supposed to have her eyes closed. Elaine slammed her eyelids shut again as she twisted back to face the front. She could feel the heat of his body radiating toward her. Inhaling, Elaine savored the scent that had surrounded Fane all day. Clean, masculine scent—no cologne or heavily perfumed body wash.

She shifted on her mat, feeling herself become wet. Elaine tried to force her mind to focus on something other than him.

"Let's begin to move," Fane instructed, moving away to stand on his mat. "Shift forward to tabletop."

Dropping athletically to his hands and knees, Fane demonstrated the posture. He led the class through a series of movements limbering up their spines.

Surely I'm not wet enough that they can see, am I? Elaine peeked behind her to see if the person behind her was looking at her display. She turned back around and met Fane's puzzled expression.

"Sorry!" she mouthed.

It's dark. No one can tell.

His slow movements intensified. The class rose to their feet to follow Fane's directions, flowing from one pose to another in a long, drawn-out procession. What seemed like very easy positions to hold caused sweat to bead on her brow as they held still for several minutes. Her muscles trembled under the effort and Elaine welcomed Fane's touch that shifted her slightly into the correct alignment. His adjustments didn't make anything easier, but they did feel better. Her snug clothing fit the practice perfectly. Even when in an upside-down vee called downward dog, her shirt remained in place and her pants didn't sag.

"It's time for our peak pose. We are going to begin working on Crow."

Several groans echoed around her. Elaine looked around apprehensively. A whisper of a notification sounded from the back corner of the room. Someone's phone had just buzzed. Her gaze fixed on Sharon as the former admin shifted off her mat.

Rolling it clumsily, Sharon looked up to call a soft, "Sorry!" to the class before flipping it over in a messy bundle and standing. Her hand closed on Knox's shoulder briefly when he moved to rise as well. The large man nodded and stilled on his mat.

Fane spoke, drawing everyone's attention back to the front of the room as he launched into an explanation of the pose, almost covering the soft closing sound of the door. Elaine focused on Fane's words as he walked the class through the steps to achieve the arm balance.

As she watched, Fane moved from a squat with his hands braced on the floor to lifting his feet. His weight balanced on his widely spread fingers as his shins pressed into the backs of his arms. He hovered with his toes off the floor as he spoke of using one's core to achieve the pose.

Elaine looked at him and nodded her acceptance of the challenge. She'd not reached her position in Edgewater Industries by taking the easy route. If he could do this, so could she.

Immediately, she threw her body into the position and fell forward, only catching herself at the last moment with a hasty preventative move of her hand before her face. *What?* He'd made it look so easy. She tried again, and this time caught herself on one forearm.

"Stop trying to force the pose, Elaine. This takes practice. Most students attempt Crow numerous times before their mind and body connect to make it possible," Fane warned her in a soft, intimate tone.

"Let's get the first step down." He walked her through the beginning steps and left her to practice lifting her hips with her core muscles instead of trying to brute force balance herself with her arms.

Continuing to practice doggedly, Elaine was determined to master the position. She glanced around herself to assess everyone else's progress. Sarah's face was red and covered with sweat. As she watched, Elaine saw Sarah lift one foot from the floor before collapsing back down on the mat.

"I did it! I got one foot up!" she announced triumphantly.

Those around her paused in their attempts to celebrate with her. They encouraged her to try again. This time Fane stood behind her as she repeated the exciting success.

"That's it! You're getting it. Remember to squeeze your knees in tight to support you. That second foot will wave in the air soon," he encouraged and laughed kindly as Sarah collapsed to the mat. "And breathe. You can't stop breathing."

"I'll remember that someday," Sarah gasped.

Elaine kept at it until Fane circled back around and smoothed a hand over her back. She looked up at him, frustrated. "I can't get it."

"You're exhausted. Stop for now. Give yourself some time to learn more and it will be possible," he counseled.

"I don't give up," she said, shaking her head.

"You're not giving up. You're waiting to practice another day."

Looking around, she noticed many people sitting patiently on their mats while the last few participants tried Crow again. Elaine shifted to sit cross-legged. She watched Fane resume his spot on his mat.

He led them through the last stretches of class to corpse pose. As everyone relaxed on their mat, Elaine struggled to keep herself awake. A few random snores and snorts attested to others facing a similar challenge. Tilting her head up, she met Fane's gaze as he sat monitoring the class. A warm feeling filled her abdomen—not arousal, but a sentiment of being cared for. Fane watched over her. She liked it a lot.

CHAPTER 5

The participants had rolled their mats up after class had ended, speaking softly to each other. While Fane was busy chatting with class members, she'd retrieved her business clothes from the locker. Not able to face changing out of the stretchy yoga gear for the tailored outfit, Elaine draped her office attire over her arm and emerged from the locker room.

Fane waited for her, lounging against the adjacent wall. The snug yoga clothes highlighted his athletic build even more in the brighter light. He pushed away and fell into step next to her.

They walked in silence to the elevator. As they waited for a car to arrive, she commented, "Class was interesting. I didn't expect that you would be the teacher."

"How does your body feel?" he asked.

The weirdly worded question made her focus. Elaine shrugged her shoulders and rotated her head. Before she could answer, the doors opened and they stepped inside. Automatically, she pressed her hand to the pad to select her floor. Fane pushed the lobby button.

When the elevator started, she answered, "Good. I feel good." The truth startled her. Most of the tension had drained from her muscles.

"Perfect. I'm glad."

When her floor appeared, she stepped out and turned to look at Fane. "Thank you." She waved a hand over her clothing. "I'll pay you back tomorrow."

"No need. Daddies enjoy taking care of Littles."

The door had closed between them before she could answer. After walking the short distance to her apartment, Elaine unlocked her door and entered. Grabbing an apple and a couple of cheese sticks, she munched her light dinner as she hung up her clothes and removed her makeup. She peeled her yoga clothes off and placed them in the laundry basket, vowing to order more.

Fane's handsome face ricocheted into her mind. Even now, staring into the mirror, her mouth rounded into a shocked expression. He didn't mean… Did he?

By the time she'd showered and brushed her teeth, Elaine had convinced herself she'd misheard. She searched her brain for an alternative that sounded like, "Daddies enjoy taking care of Littles."

Maybe he'd said, "Doesn't taking care of the little (things)."

Okay, that's ridiculous. No one would say that. He doesn't know, does he? No, he can't. That's crazy.

Maybe… Didn't you enjoy tackling Crow a little? Oh, that makes perfect sense. He was talking about yoga.

After turning off the lights, she climbed into bed to watch the market report for the day. As she got settled in the soft bedding, Elaine hugged and kissed her childhood stuffie, who waited on her pillow. Ballsy's fur had faded over the years. The lines representing his shell now blended into a muddled hue. In Elaine's eyes, he was as beautiful as he had always been.

She'd never admit to still sleeping with the stuffed animal in public. People wouldn't understand. Elaine knew how important he was. Just because she got bigger didn't mean Ballsy wasn't family anymore. Besides, it was Ballsy who always reminded her to go to sleep when she became too embroiled in the business reports on TV.

* * *

ELAINE TOOK care to dress in her most professional attire and applied more makeup than usual to create the image she wanted to project. Picking up the briefcase she never needed to use, she power walked across the lobby and across the green space to building A.

With a breezy good morning to staff members as she passed them, Elaine headed directly to her office to tackle the last of the report. Pausing in the doorway, she glimpsed Fane at his desk with his cuffs rolled up. Her gaze traced the colorful tattoos, reminding her of his appearance in last night's revealing yoga clothes. She'd never be able to forget that.

"Good morning, Fane. No interruptions, please. I will finish the reports today," she declared, setting her expectation for the day.

"Got it, boss. Consider me your guard dog."

"Thank you, Fane."

Elaine turned to walk into her office and jumped when a deep-throated bark sounded behind her. Whirling to stare at her admin, Elaine was at a total loss for words.

"Woof!" Fane repeated the low sound with a grin.

Shaking her head, Elaine proceeded into her office. Settling at her desk, she powered on her laptop and dove into the report. When Fane intervened after a couple of hours, she allowed him to take her to the rooftop garden for a breath of fresh air. Thankfully, he remained quiet, allowing her to continue to think through the data that she had compiled.

"That's it!" she announced, whirling away from the breathtaking view at the building's edge. "I knew I was missing something."

Without thinking, she grabbed his hand and tugged Fane back to the elevator. Words tumbled from her mouth. "Fane, we're missing the key piece. There's a report somewhere in my office that details the surveyor's report of the new property Edgewater Industries is considering for development. I know there are some additional benefits that I'm missing in the report."

"Do you remember the name of the surveying company?"

"It wasn't our normal partner. I went outside the regular paths of information to keep this under wraps. I also wanted to check that the reports we had been getting were valid."

"You were suspicious?"

"Not for any definitive reasons," she admitted as the elevator opened on their floor.

"But something had alerted your spidey senses?" he asked with an arched eyebrow as they walked toward their offices.

"Yes. I didn't think a lot of it when the report came through, but I think something has clicked into place now that I'm pulling together all the pieces for the report."

"Let's find it. Are we searching for paper or electronic forms?" Fane looked around the reception area at the neatly organized file cabinets he'd worked hard to pull together.

"Both. Can you look for a hard copy while I search the files on my computer?"

Fane held out his hand, palm down. When she looked at him in confusion, he commented, "You never played football, huh?"

"No?" she admitted, bewildered by the change in topic.

Undeterred, Fane took one of her hands and placed it over his, still extended in the air. He cupped his free hand over hers, sandwiching her hand between his, as he nodded at her other arm. When she tentatively placed hers on top, he bounced the stack up and down repeatedly, ending with one final push downward.

"Go, Team!" he cheered.

When Elaine stared at him dumbfounded, he waved her toward her office. Obeying, she turned to peek at him over her shoulder and stumbled before catching herself. Fane, bent over a file drawer, was a very distracting view. Shaking her errant thoughts away, Elaine forced herself into her office and joined the search.

* * *

"Mark where you are," Fane instructed from the doorway two hours later. "It's time for lunch."

"I'll get something later," she answered absentmindedly.

"Nope. Now."

Looking up at him, Elaine commented dismissively and underlined her words as she pointed to each of them. "Boss, employee."

Fane shook his head and walked over to the office door. Closing the barrier, he locked it before turning back to face her. "Last chance to take a break that you know you need."

"Later." She waved a hand at him before turning back to her laptop.

Elaine felt his presence next to her before he rolled her chair from under the desk. She pressed her heels into the carpet and regretted taking off her uncomfortable pumps when the rough fibers rug-burned her skin. Instantly, she raised her feet to avoid getting hurt as he whisked the office chair to face one of the guest chairs in front of her desk.

"I'm busy," she protested as he sat mere inches away from her.

"You're always busy, Little girl. You also have a short memory. Do you remember how much you accomplished yesterday when you got away from this office for a while?"

"Don't you mean boss?" she said, narrowing her eyes as she strove to prevent herself from panicking at the words 'Little girl.' *He can't know.*

"No. I spoke correctly," Fane answered easily. "We're going to set up some guidelines, Elaine."

"When I finish the report, we can discuss anything you wish to discuss pertaining to work and your position here."

As if ignoring her protests of business, Fane countered, "The last thing we need to talk about is work. You're incredible in your position and I have professional skills that can support and enable you as you accomplish your work goals. When is the report due?"

"I have to get it to Easton the day before the meeting. So, the last possible moment is in two days. That doesn't matter. I want to get this done today."

"We're setting the deadline for two days. There's nothing that says you can't finish today, but we have to find that document. That requires me stumbling across it, or you remembering something to help us find it."

"So, we need to look—not take a break."

"I will not allow you to stress yourself into an early grave."

Elaine stared at him. Seconds passed by. "You are not in control. The last time I checked, my name is posted outside that door and in the lobby with Chief Operating Officer next to it. Not yours."

"Oh, you're in charge of the company," he agreed.

"Then, our discussion is over." Putting her feet on the carpet, Elaine prepared to scoot herself behind her desk.

"What?" she squeaked, clutching his broad shoulders as he lifted her easily from the office chair to set her on his lap.

"Little girl, you may be the boss when the door is open. When we're alone, the Daddy inside me will take whatever action is needed to safeguard you. Whether that is spanking your bottom for failing to take care of yourself or this." His hand cupped the back of her head to pull her close.

She froze as his lips brushed hers softly. Fluttering her eyelids closed to focus on the delicious sensation, Elaine leaned closer to deepen the kiss. In response, he ran his tongue over the seam of her lips, requesting her to allow him inside. With a gasp, Elaine opened her mouth.

Masterfully, Fane tasted her. His kisses were slow and deep as he sought to bring her pleasure. Focused completely on her, the powerful man tightened his arms around her to hug her against his hard body. Once she was tethered close to him with one arm, he moved his other arm to caress the length of her spine.

Unable to resist the exquisite touch, Elaine arched her back under his stimulating strokes. As if ruled by someone else, her hands crept over his sculpted muscles during his sensual exploration to wrap around his neck. She pushed all contradicting thoughts from her mind.

I want this bad.

"Damn, Little girl," he murmured against her lips. He leaned back slightly to rip off his steamed-up glasses and toss them onto her desk before dipping his tongue inside to taste her again.

She wanted to be embarrassed by their heated passion, but inside, a flame of delight flared higher. Fane was as into her as she was attracted to him. Elaine tugged at the short hair at the nape of his neck as she clung to him. Just a few more kisses and she'd force herself to stop.

When he cupped her bottom with that caressing hand, she pulled back to look at him. Trying to control the bewildered expression she knew was reflected in her eyes, Elaine stared at him. What was happening?

"I know, Laney." Fane weaved his fingers through her thick hair, pushing the strands behind one ear. "This is happening very quickly for you, Little girl. It's scary and exciting at the same time."

"Why do you keep calling me Little girl?"

Fane kissed her lips in a feather-light touch that somehow seemed more intensive. "I won't let you lie to me," he warned.

When she started to reply, he pressed his lips to hers once again before requesting, "Let me talk first."

She could only nod her consent.

"Good girl. We both know that people's insides and outsides don't always match. The most aggressive pro wrestler could be sexually submissive. The least outgoing person could be a masterful Dom who demands everything."

Fane waited for her to nod once again. "No one needs to know that secret person inside except the one individual who can make those secret desires come true."

"I don't…"

"I get to talk first, right?"

"Yes, but…"

"Me first. Then I will listen to you, Laney."

She nodded.

"I knew I was different from other guys my age early. There was a part of me that wanted to care for people—not everyone, just certain individuals. Something in them drew me. When I hit puberty, it became more obvious. As I explored different lifestyles, I discovered who I was."

Elaine wanted to ask but couldn't. She stayed quiet, hoping he would continue.

"I have a feeling it took a while for you to figure it out, too. Your brilliant mind would not have rested until you put the pieces together. My bet was you found a book that captivated you. One that you returned to read over and over until you couldn't deny that you were that character. That you are a Little."

Shaking her head instantly to deny his words, Elaine froze as he continued.

"You know that about yourself, just as I know I am a Daddy. When I discovered you two years ago, I knew instantly."

"What did you know?"

"That the strong, incredibly intelligent woman who helps lead Edgewater Industries to increasing levels of success is my Little."

"I didn't know you two years ago." She grasped at that detail to deny he was right.

"You didn't. I had recently transferred here to take a position as an admin. I always work hard. That's who I am. But when I heard you address the company, I knew I needed to gain the higher-level skills required to be your personal assistant."

"But I hadn't ever met you?" she protested, searching her memory for a previous encounter with him.

"No. You and I weren't ready for each other. Now, we are."

"Maybe you've made a mistake," she proposed to camouflage herself.

"Everyone makes mistakes, but this isn't one of mine. You are my Little, Laney, and I am your Daddy. Put aside your position and my position. There's no one here but us. Can you be brave and search your mind and heart? Can you feel it, too?"

Elaine didn't have a clue what to say. Her whole life seemed to be in jeopardy. What would he do if she admitted something so personal?

"You have my promise, Laney, that I will never hurt you professionally, and that I'll try my damnedest not to hurt you personally. I am going to push you to admit what you're hiding and to allow me to take care of you. Stop thinking so hard and just feel."

His powerful hands drew her back against his chest. Holding her close, Fane gently rocked back and forth as he rubbed her back.

Hiding her face in the crook of his neck, Elaine struggled to push all the dire what-ifs out of her whirling mind. The heat of his body seeped into hers, warming her tight muscles. Fane's quiet strength reassured her on the most basic level. Could she trust him enough? He'd never given her any negative indications.

"I'm not calling you Daddy," she finally whispered.

"You will," he contradicted, squeezing her tight. "Ready to take a break? I have something to show you."

"Okay." She grasped at a distraction. Elaine needed something to hide behind. Allowing him to set her back in her office chair, she held onto the armrests with a tight grip as he scooted the chair back behind the desk.

"Save your work," he instructed and kissed the top of her head when she followed his directions. "Now, a break!"

CHAPTER 6

Wearing the perfectly sized sneakers that Fane had produced from somewhere, Elaine followed him out of the building and into the sunshine. She watched the reactions of the employees milling about during their normal activities. *Does anyone suspect?*

No one seemed to look at her differently. Everyone greeted them with the familiar ease that showcased the collegial environment at Edgewater Industries. Elaine tried to relax.

"No one cares, Laney."

Elaine looked at him in surprise. "Do you think they know?"

"Everyone that works here knows you put in more hours and effort than everyone but Easton himself. You're respected by all, even the admins who've worked for you. That says a lot when you've scared the crap out of them."

"I didn't really," she protested. "They just couldn't stay up with my pace."

Fane laughed and patted her on the lower back as he steered her toward the path leading toward the edge of the property. "I have a surprise for you."

"I don't think I like surprises," she countered, overwhelmed by all that had happened in her life already today.

They entered a small clearing. A massive tree majestically commanded the spotlight in the center of the open space. Its branches spread in all directions, causing the sunlight to filter through the leaves. Sparkling beams penetrated the shade and created an almost fairytale atmosphere.

"Wow! I didn't know this was here." Elaine turned in a circle as they reached the center of the cleared space.

"I like to hike along the border of the property after hours. When I discovered this area, I could see the potential even though it was entrenched in weeds and brambles. A bunch of residents of B tower and their Daddies worked hard to create this amazing place."

"Their Daddies?" Elaine repeated.

"I'm sure you know that B Tower has special housing for the Littles who work for the company, and that Easton has a soft spot for Littles and wants to protect you all."

She seized on those words, 'you all.' "Me? Easton knows about me?" Elaine squeaked, panicking once again.

Fane pulled her close and hugged her. "Elaine, are your professional abilities any different today than they were a week ago?"

"No."

"Have you changed your dedication to supporting and expanding Edgewater Industries in the last fifteen minutes?"

"Of course not! That's ridiculous," she snorted against his shoulder.

"Did your Little status come up in any meeting with Easton about the company or your performance as the second in command—ever?"

"No." Elaine took a deep breath and blew it out raggedly. "He knows I'm Little."

"Yes."

"How?"

"He's a Daddy. He's been looking for his Little for a very long time. Now that he's found her, Easton wants everyone to find their happily ever after. That's why he allowed me to step in as your admin."

"Piper?" Elaine answered as her brain put the pieces together.

"Come sit down and swing." Fane guided her to the plain flat seat suspended by smooth ropes looped over a massive, nearly horizontal branch of the massive oak.

Her mind busy, she complied with his guidance and soon glided back and forth in the fresh air. Enchanted, Elaine tried to memorize this place. The magical setting calmed her soul and settled her mind as if the breeze whisked away her errant thoughts and worries. Fane stood behind her, gently pushing the swing. She couldn't see him, but could sense his presence. With a start, she realized that having him near made her happy.

"Fane?"

"Yes, Laney."

"No one's ever called me that. I've always been Elaine."

"Then I'm the first. That makes me happy. Do you like the name Laney?"

"I do. It's fun. It sounds Little."

"I think it matches you well."

She nodded and swung back and forth in silence a few times. The next trip backward, Elaine turned again to meet his gaze as she went by. Forcing herself to be brave, she asked, "You said you knew I was yours for a while. Why didn't you say anything?"

"You weren't ready. And to be honest, I wasn't either. Now, I'm able to support your career and your heart."

"I don't think I can be your Little girl at work. That would have to be completely separate to keep people from knowing and losing respect for me," Elaine blurted.

"Being Little isn't something you play at during your time off. Nor is being a Daddy. I promise I will honor the position that you have worked hard to earn. You are the expert in business and Edgewater's path forward."

"Great! You won't tell me what to do at work," she said happily, swinging her feet to go faster.

Then it dawned on her. "Wait! You're already telling what to do at work!" She lowered her feet to scuff the earth below her to slow down.

"I'm making sure you take care of yourself. I'm not telling you how to do your job. There's an enormous difference," Fane pointed out.

It took several swings back and forth to come to an eventual stop. It wasn't like she could jump out of the seat like she was flying while wearing a straight skirt. By the time she could stand, Elaine had digested his words.

"There is a difference. But, there also could be a conflict when the two collide—when my work obligations crash into your efforts to take care of me," she pointed out.

"Then we talk."

"Is it that easy?"

"It is. Ready to head back?" Fane asked, holding out his hand for hers.

Slipping her fingers between his, she smiled before answering, "Yes."

Halfway back, she abruptly yanked Fane to a stop and turned to face him. A few other employees walked along the paths they were on now. They simply streamed around them.

Grinning with satisfaction, Elaine announced, "I know the name of the company."

"I knew you'd come up with the information you needed. Let's go find it!" Fane squeezed her hand as he stared at her mouth.

Elaine knew he wished to kiss her but was restraining himself. Bouncing forward, she lifted onto her toes and gave him a kiss. This relationship was either the best thing ever or the worst. As his arms wrapped around her, she decided to treasure the memories they made together for as long as her Daddy would put up with her.

* * *

THAT AFTERNOON, she typed the last words of her report. Sending the entire document to Easton in advance, she pushed back her chair. Silently celebrating, Elaine shot her arms into the air.

Fane called from the doorway, "Looks like you're ready. Come on, the wind is perfect and it's after five. Work's over. It's time to play."

He moved slightly away to show her a massive kite in his hands. "Want to go fly Ollie?"

"Is that an octopus?" she asked, incredulous of the streamers flowing over his arms in a riot of colors.

"Of course! What else could Ollie be? A giraffe?" he joked.

Laughing at his assumption that an octopus made a much more appropriate kite than a giraffe could, Elaine jumped to her feet. "I think we deserve a bit of time off while Easton reviews the report. I'll warn you, I don't think I've ever flown a kite before."

"Then it's high time you did. You need to change into play clothes. Jeans and sneakers are required for this activity," he commented, looking over her professional pencil skirt, blouse, and high heels.

"Let me turn off my computer," Elaine said, whirling around to hit the power button on her computer.

A few minutes later, they rushed into the elevator with the large kite cradled in their arms to avoid it dragging on the floor. Fane carried the heavy spool of string.

"We won't need that much line, will we?" Elaine asked, staring at the neatly wound spindle.

"It depends on the wind. Ollie is made to soar way over the campus area. Everyone should be able to see it."

"You've never flown it before?" she asked, studying his face.

"A quick test flight to make sure I had the line attached correctly. I only put it up about ten feet into the air. The tentacles were dragging on the ground when it dipped and soared. Ollie's had a taste of flying and is eager to coast above us."

"I can't wait to see it," Elaine marveled, stretching one tentacle out as far as her arm would reach. She tried to maintain her professional demeanor but bounced up and down eagerly on her toes.

They dashed across the green space between the A and B Towers. In the lobby, Knox looked up from his computer to greet them.

"Hey, you two. Guess you survived yoga," he joked with a rare smile.

"I did. We're waiting for Easton to review the quarterly report so…" Elaine's voice drifted off as she lifted the colorful material in her hands.

"That looks like fun," he commented. "Elaine, do you want me to add Fane to your list of approved visitors?"

As her face heated, Elaine nodded. "Please, Knox."

"Got it. Fane, press your hand to the sensor when you get to the elevator. I'll update your clearance to add Elaine's floor to your current ability to access the gym level."

"Thank you, Knox." Fane steered Elaine to the elevator and, in a flurry of nylon, freed one hand to press against the panel. Immediately, elevator doors opened to welcome them.

Elaine noted Fane's nod of appreciation to Knox as they stepped inside. "Do you think he knows?"

"Knox is aware of everything. You don't have to worry about him revealing any secrets. The information in his brain is locked down as tight as… well, Fort Knox."

"He's a Daddy too, isn't he?"

"He is," Fane confirmed. "He knows who his Little is as well."

"Who is it?"

"That's Knox's business, Laney. You'll know some day. Come on, lead me to your apartment. Ollie's getting impatient," Fane shared, playacting that the kite was getting restless in his arms.

"I'm in 621. It's this way."

Elaine led him down one hallway and to the left. Many of the apartments they passed had decorated doors, making it festive as they passed. When she stopped in front of hers, Elaine apologized for the lack of adornments.

"Mine is the plain door. I never have time to keep switching everything around. I tried at first but didn't get the winter decorations down until May."

"I'll have to confess my door doesn't showcase a seasonal display either. I'm sure your neighbors don't mind. Some people enjoy putting things up for fun," he assured her.

"Come on in. It will just take me a minute to change."

Opening the door, Elaine stepped in first to make sure the apartment was in the neat order that she always maintained it. Nodding when she found it acceptable, she turned to Fane and asked, "Shall we put Ollie on the couch to rest before we take him out?"

"Good idea."

After settling the streaming bits across the seat cushions, Elaine said, "My apartment is pretty small. You can see most of it. The kitchen is on the left and my bedroom and bathroom are through that doorway."

"It's a perfect size for one Little girl. Let's get you changed." Fane held out a hand for hers.

"You're going to help me?" she squeaked, instantly squeezing her legs together.

"No, Laney. You're going to help me," he corrected. "Daddies always dress their Littles. Go choose your favorite jeans and a T-shirt from your closet."

Glad to have a task to focus on, Elaine rushed into her bedroom and into the closet. She pulled two garments from the tidy arrangement of hangers and darted back into her room. There she found Fane standing at the bottom of her bed. Tracing his gaze back to her pillows, she knew he saw the two stuffies lying on the bed—one blue bunny and one gray bug with antennae.

"I wondered where he went. I didn't see you leave with him."

"Blueberry was lonely in my desk, so I brought him home to play with Ballsy," she explained.

"Ballsy is a…"

"Roly poly, or if you prefer, a pill bug, *Armadillidium vulgarare*." She pronounced the Latin phrase with the ease of someone who memorized that pronunciation years ago.

"Ballsy. The perfect name because he rolls up in a ball." Fane smiled at her. "Are the two playing nicely together?"

"They are best friends," she assured him.

"What do they talk about?" he asked as he turned her around to face him. Fane began to unfasten the pearl-toned buttons as she answered.

"Um, they talk about me and other fun stuff," Elaine faltered as he undressed her. "I can do that."

"Daddy's job."

"This is hard," she whispered as her shirt sagged away from her body.

"You are a beautiful Little girl, Laney," he assured her as he gently pulled her shirt from her waistband before sliding her top from her shoulders and off her arms.

After draping it over her bed, he pressed a soft kiss to her lips. "I'm attracted to your shapely adult body as much as I treasure the Little inside you. Okay to continue?" he asked.

"Yes, Daddy," she whispered. Her mind drifted automatically into Little space as his hands touched her body.

"Good girl," he praised. Fane guided her to turn away from him and he efficiently unfastened her slim skirt and allowed it to drop to the floor. Scooping her up in his arms, Fane sat her on the bed to remove her high heels.

When Elaine wrapped her arms around her torso, shielding her body from his view, Fane firmly pressed her arms to her sides. "No hiding from Daddy."

"No hiding from Daddy," Laney repeated as she tucked her fingertips under her thighs to keep herself from repeating the action.

"That's my sweet Little girl."

Fane rewarded her with a warm kiss that sent shockwaves through her body. *He's the best kisser ever!* Laney responded to him eagerly, wishing his kisses would never end.

When he stroked down her side to cup her hip, Laney pulled back slightly to meet his gaze. The heat reflected in his eyes fueled the arousal that had already been building inside her since they entered her apartment. She knew he wanted her as much as she was drawn to him.

"Are your panties wet, Laney? We'll need to change them before we put on your jeans if they are."

She shook her head vigorously to deny this possibility.

"Spread your legs so I can check," he directed, gliding his fingers over the material stretched around her in a feather-light touch that made her inner thighs clench automatically. He waited patiently for her to follow his directions.

Slowly, Laney eased her thighs apart. She held her breath as his fingers traced the seam between her lower lips to her core. Those tantalizing fingers brushed back and forth across the gusset of her panties. Watching that intimate caress that sent shivers through her body, she glanced up at his face to find him watching her.

"I think we need to change these panties as well."

She could only nod her agreement. Laney couldn't argue with the proof of her desire soaking the soft material.

"Lie back, Little girl," Fane instructed, helping support her back as she settled against the mattress.

"Lift your hips." His fingers hooked into the sides of her panties and drew them downward.

Automatically, she pressed down with her heels, raising her bottom from the comforter. Laney lowered herself down as she felt the material reach her mid-thigh. She closed her eyes as he drew them to her ankles before sliding them off. Immediately, she drew her legs together.

His hands pressed her thighs apart. Opening her eyes, Laney looked at him in surprise. She bit her bottom lip as his fingers traced the seam of her pussy. When he lifted them from her body, she could see her juices shining on his skin. Slowly, he removed his black glasses to set them to the side.

"Daddy needs to make sure his Little is okay," Fane shared before asking softly, "Have you been tested lately?"

When she quickly nodded, he whispered, "Me, too. I wanted to make sure I kept you safe and healthy. I had the health center run a test the week before I started working for you."

"Me, too," Laney answered in a barely audible tone. "I mean it's been a long time... since I was... with anyone. I did get tested afterward."

Laney watched Fane press a warm kiss to her inner thigh. She curled her fingers into the soft comforter below her as he lowered his head between her legs. His warm breath on her most intimate space made her close her eyes once again. Needing to hide and wanting to block everything out except for his touch, Laney held her breath as she heard him inhale.

"Mmm, Little girl," he murmured, lowering his head to taste her.

Squirming at the first touch of his tongue, Laney felt his hands span her inner thighs to pin her in place. She froze, trying not to strain up toward his mouth in her eagerness. Thankfully, he didn't make her wait long. Savoring her flavor with obvious enjoyment, her Daddy explored her pink folds, repeating his caresses to sensitive spots as she responded to him.

He lifted one hand from her thigh to explore her body. After tracing a fingertip around her soaked opening to circle that small bud hidden above, Fane pushed her arousal higher by sealing his lips around the sensitive bundle of nerves and sucking lightly. Laney moaned in delight as two fingers slid into her, stretching her tight passage slightly.

His caresses continued to build her arousal. She could feel her orgasm building until it shimmered just outside of her grasp. When his mouth lifted from her body, Laney automatically protested, "No!" before stuffing her hands into her mouth in embarrassment.

"Let Daddy hear your sweet sounds, Laney," he requested before lowering his mouth to nibble at her gently.

That was the last bit she needed. Her body exploded into an avalanche of excitement at the hint of pain, clamping around his inserted fingers. She screamed her pleasure into the room, shuddering underneath him as he stroked her, prolonging the sensations that echoed through her. Laney melted onto the bed when he lifted his head again and eased his fingers away.

Fane rose from his position of kneeling between her legs to lie next to her on the bed. Gathering her in his arms, he held her close while he rocked her softly. "That's my good girl. Thank you for trusting your Daddy to make you feel good."

She nestled into his shoulder, enjoying their intimacy. Not knowing what to say, Laney chose to let her Daddy guide her in this uncharted territory. After a few minutes, he kissed her forehead, drawing her from her thoughts.

"Go potty, Laney. Daddy will follow you in a couple of minutes to help you get cleaned up for fresh clothes."

Curling away from him reluctantly, Laney stood. Feeling embarrassed by wearing her bra and nothing else, she scurried to the bathroom and peed quickly. As she flushed the toilet, he appeared in the doorway.

"Washcloth?" he asked.

Laney pointed to the cabinet under the sink. He opened the door to select a fluffy scrap of cloth. Turning on the warm water, Fane waved her over in front of him as he set it down on the vanity.

"Come wash your hands, Laney. Daddy will help you." As she moved to stand between him and the sink, Fane pressed a kiss to her neck.

Reaching forward to wet her hands, she paused as he squirted some fragrant soap into his hand. Fane rubbed his larger hands over hers, sudsing the lather over her skin. "Sing the ABC song, Laney. Then we'll know when the germs are all gone."

His warm baritone filled the small space. "A, B, C, D, E, F…"

She jumped in to join him in her soft alto at the letter G and together they finished the song. Laney allowed him to guide her hands into the stream of warm water and giggled as the bubbles disappeared down the drain.

"Go dry your hands, cutie," he instructed with another kiss that made her giggle more.

As she turned toward the towel rack, Laney watched him dunk the washcloth into the warm water. She put together his words. *He's going to wash me next!*

"I can do it," she assured him as he approached with the damp cloth.

"Daddy's job," he corrected. Without a smidgen of a hesitation, Fane quickly wiped between her legs. He cleaned the tops of her inner thighs as well before pulling the towel from the rack to dry her skin.

"One last place to rinse," he told her with a wink as he turned to the sink to splash water over his lower face before drying it with the towel.

His low laugh reassured her when she felt her face flame with embarrassment. "I'd rather leave your scent on me."

"Daddy!" she protested.

"Come on, Laney. Ollie has waited patiently for us to get you changed. Let's go." He ushered her back into the bedroom and, without a fuss, helped her into her clothing and shoes.

When she was ready, he piled some of Ollie's tentacles into her hands and ushered her to the door. "Let's go fly a kite."

In just a few minutes, they were choosing the best green space to set Ollie free. "There's a tree over there. I don't want to hurt Ollie. How about here?"

"Perfect! Let's get him stretched out," Fane suggested.

With that task accomplished, he curled Laney's fingers around the support on the back of the kite. "Hold this up over your head and run. Let go when the wind catches it."

"Run?" she double-checked.

"Like the wind," he encouraged with a grin as he let out string.

"Ahhhh!" She turned and raced away from him, feeling the air wrap under the kite and tug at it. After a few more steps, she let go and clapped her hands to celebrate as it climbed into the sky.

"It's flying!" she cheered.

"Come help me feed out the line. Let's see if we can get it higher than the top office up there," Fane invited. He lifted one arm to let her scoot between his outstretched arms.

Steadily adding more line, Laney leaned back against Fane as she studied it in the sky. There were a few heart-rending moments as it looked like Ollie would crash to the ground, but her incredible Daddy yanked back on the spool to lift it back into the air. Soon, all the tentacles were waving festively in the air as a crowd gathered on the edges of the green space to point and delight at the display.

"Way to go, Ms. Rivers! Fane!" reached her ears, and she smiled at the crowd. She liked that they were celebrating with her. At times, she'd felt outside the close-knit community as a participant, but not really a member.

"This is so much fun!" she cheered over her shoulder.

"Daddies always know how to make their Littles smile," he whispered privately. "I love to see you happy."

Elaine realized in just the few short days since Fane had been her assistant, she had already smiled more than she had in months. "Thank you."

"You're welcome," he assured her with a discreet hug as she settled back in the circle of his arms. "Look! Ollie's made it over the top of the building. Think anyone is up there watching him wave?"

"I hope so!"

CHAPTER 7

"Can we fly Ollie again?" Laney asked as they sat in her apartment around the coffee table, eating the pizza delivery Knox had on speed dial. She'd seen their trucks arrive many times from her window, but never ordered. It seemed too lonely to have a pizza delivered just for one.

"I think he'd like that. What do you think of the pizza?" Fane asked, lifting a piece of cheese pizza out of the box to place on her plate as they comfortably sat in her living area.

"I love it. Even the crust is good," she answered, popping the last of her previous piece into her mouth.

"Knox knows his stuff," Fane answered as he helped himself to another piece as well. Opening the small packet of dried red peppers that had come with the delivery, he sprinkled them liberally over the still warm cheese.

"Isn't that too hot?" she blurted.

"I like everything with a bit of spice," he assured her with a suggestive raised eyebrow.

Laney tried to ignore the heat that built in her face at his implication. Quickly, she took another bite of pizza. Chewing, she gathered her courage. Finally, after swallowing, she made herself ask, "What do you see happening between us?"

"I see you moving into your nursery in my house and making it our home. I want to walk with you to work every day, make sure you take care of yourself as diligently as you work for the company, and tuck you into bed each night with a smile on your face."

She stared at his easy, open answer. "It's that easy?"

"It is. Just as easy as it was for you to call me Daddy," he teased.

"I didn't mean to do that. It just felt right."

"I think if we're both honest, being together feels righter than anything else."

Laney nodded without needing to examine her feelings. It was a complete no-brainer. She enjoyed being with Fane even when he didn't do what she wanted him to. Her Daddy definitely didn't let her control him.

"So where do we go from here?"

"We set up guidelines to help us both get what we need from the relationship."

"Like what kind of guidelines?"

"Do you have a pad of paper here?" he asked. When she nodded, he added, "Go get it and a few pens or markers."

Taking another bite, Laney jumped up from the floor in front of the low table and ran to her desk to grab some paper from a drawer. Another drawer yielded a handful of markers in different colors. "Are we going to make a to-do list?"

"Yes. Let's make two lists. You write down the things you'd like to have your Daddy do for you. I'll detail the things I need for my Little girl to do. Then, we'll compare."

"What kind of things?" Laney asked, placing a piece of paper in front of each of them and offering him a choice of writing implements. Even after their intimacy earlier, she didn't want to reveal more than he was suggesting.

"I'm going to add one thing to your list to start you out. We can take it off if you don't agree." Fane pulled her page in front and selected a blue marker.

Daddy and Laney will experiment to determine how Little Laney needs to be.

He scooted the page in front of her and waited.

Laney reread the phrase several times. Each time, she wanted to ask what he meant, but wasn't brave enough. Finally, she peeked up at him.

"Use your words, Laney. We have to be able to talk."

"Can you explain this to me?" she blurted.

"Littles come in all shapes and sizes. They also identify best at different ages. Can you tell me definitively how old the Little inside you is? Are you a baby, a toddler, a teenager, or somewhere in between?"

"I don't know," she whispered.

"Neither do I. I see all of those in you at different times. That's what we may find after we experiment. Sometimes, you need to be very Little in Daddy's arms and others you need to be more independent but with boundaries."

"So, we try different things out and see what happens?" Laney asked.

"Yes."

"I think I'd like that," she agreed.

"I know I'd like that, too. Now, you add those things you want," he directed.

Pulling the cap off a green marker, Laney bent over her budding list. She wrote one line and then scratched out a word to replace it with an alternative above it before choosing another color for the next addition. Casually stretching one arm around her page, she guarded it from his view, just like she had kept her answers from classmates who would have copied from her. Laney knew he noticed when he glanced over, but he didn't say a word. His page remained open to her view.

Daddy is in charge.
Daddy needs Laney's care and affection, too.
Daddy will always be watching.

Fane took another bite of pizza and sat back to review his list. He

PEPPER NORTH

picked up his marker and changed the last one to sound less ominous.

Daddy will always be watching, so he can take the best care of Laney possible.

The smile on his face indicated he was more satisfied with that one. Leaning back against the cushions on her couch, he munched on the rest of his slice as he looked out the window. She knew he was giving her time and privacy to finish hers.

"Is that all you're going to add?" she asked.

"Sometimes less is more. We can always adjust things if we need to."

"My list is going to be longer."

"That's okay. You write what you need me to know."

After several minutes, Laney set an orange marker down. "I think I'm done."

"Do you want to talk about my list first?"

"Please." She leapt at his offer.

"Laney will listen to her Daddy. I know you will not wish to follow my directions all the time. It's important for you to know that I'm not creating things to make you jump through hoops. I'll base anything I ask you to do on what I know you need."

"Like taking breaks and drinking water?"

"Yes, and yes. But it also includes having consequences."

"What kind of consequences? Are you going to spank me?" she asked, half kidding and half apprehensive.

"Spankings and Littles go together. That's a given. But other punishments exist as well. You might have to stand in the corner. Write sentences. There are lots of options Daddies can use to capture their Littles' attention."

"I have to let you do what you want?"

"You have to trust me to know what you need," he explained softly. "Being Little means you give yourself into someone's care completely. Only you can decide whether I'm the right Daddy for you."

"Oh," she whispered. "I have a hard time relying on anyone but myself."

"I know. We have nothing but time to build that trust. You are going to have to take a leap of faith in our relationship," he gently requested.

"That leads directly into my second guideline. *Daddy needs Laney's care and affection, too.* Daddies may seem invincible, but I need to know you want to be with me as well. Eventually, I need to know you love me as much as the love I feel for you."

"You love me?"

"I do. Remember, I've been hovering at the edges of your life for a while."

"I can't tell you that now," she admitted honestly.

"I know. You will when you're ready. For now, I'm happy to see your eyes light up when I come into your office."

"The office is definitely more fun than it has been before," she laughed.

"I enjoyed our play this afternoon as well."

Instantly, she knew he wasn't referring to their time flying Ollie. "You made me feel special," she shared, standing up to lean over the table to kiss him.

Fane wrapped his hand around the back of her head to hold her steady as he deepened her light kiss into something much more. When he lifted his lips from hers, Laney sank back in her chair as she tried to gather herself. He just did something for her that no one else ever had. She laughed when he took off his steamed-up glasses to clean the lenses.

He's so handsome. And he wants me.

Fane winked at her before sliding his black frames into place. "My last is obvious. *Daddy will always be watching, so he can take the best care of Laney possible.*"

Laney nodded. She knew he was always aware of her when they were together. That statement could have sounded ominous with someone other than Fane, but with him, she welcomed his attention.

"Are you ready to share your list?"

Turning the paper toward him, Laney held her breath as he scanned the multicolored sentences.

Laney needs to know that her Daddy will always be there.

Laney will learn to follow her Daddy's directions and will accept the consequences when she makes poor choices.

Daddy will support Laney's work goals and dedication.

Daddy will help Laney enjoy life.

"I thought my list would be longer, but these pretty well sum it up," she explained when he didn't say anything for a few seconds.

"Come sit on my lap," he directed.

"Really?"

"Come here, Laney. I need to hold you."

She stood slowly and circled the coffee table that separated them. He guided her with supportive hands onto his lap. Immediately, Fane wrapped his arms around her to hold her close. Laney tilted her head to the side when he nuzzled his mouth to the sensitive skin of her neck. She shivered against him as she looked at the relationship they'd just established.

"I love that you divided this into action steps for us. I can promise you without hesitation that I want to provide everything on your list."

Fane leaned their bodies forward to align the two lists, one above the other, before sitting back up. Quietly, they considered the items delineated on each. Laney liked how they matched up but weren't the same.

Daddy is in charge.

Daddy needs Laney's care and affection, too.

Daddy will always be watching, so he can take the best care of Laney possible.

Laney needs to know that her Daddy will always be there.

Laney will learn to follow her Daddy's directions and will accept the consequences when she makes poor choices.

Daddy will support Laney's work goals and dedication.

Daddy will help Laney enjoy life.

"That looks like one list to me," he observed.

"I could have written yours as well. That's kinda scary," she said, turning to watch his face.

"I love yours. Especially the last one."

"You're good at that. I get too embroiled in work. It's easy for me to fall into a pattern of making work my life."

Fane nodded his head as he stroked his fingers through her thick brown hair. "You're going to struggle with the first one."

"Not at work, right? I'm in charge at work."

"You're in charge of our work. You are not in charge of you or me. Daddy will always make the rules," he pointed out.

"I don't understand the difference."

"You set the goals for your office. Completing reports, working with other departments, looking ahead for future growth… for all those things, you make the decisions. Ensuring that you balance work and life—that's my job. Along with being the best administrative assistant ever, of course."

"What do we do now?" she asked, waving a hand at the papers.

"It's time for you to brush your teeth and hop into bed. Tomorrow, I'd like to take you to my home to see your nursery and spend the night with Daddy."

"I'd like that."

"I would, too."

CHAPTER 8

Checking her schedule when she woke up, Elaine noted her boss had created a meeting time for them at ten. Immediately, she jumped out of bed so she could get into the office early to review the report. Had he found something negative? A mistake?

Dressed and with perfect makeup, Elaine walked through her living space toward the apartment door. At the sight of the papers on the coffee table, she paused before heading back into her bedroom to pack a small tote bag with clothes and her stuffies.

Thank goodness my best meeting outfit is wrinkle free!

Elaine walked across the campus, greeting others as she passed. From their surprised expressions, she realized that usually she was deep in thought as she started her day. She must have missed interacting with others.

Arriving at her office, she smiled at Fane and called, "Good morning."

He followed her into her private office and closed the door. "I need a kiss, Little girl. Then I'll go slog through all the stuff on my calendar for today."

She stepped eagerly into his arms. As usual, Fane's kisses kindled a fire deep inside her stomach. Elaine pressed herself against his hard body, trying to get as close to him as possible.

"You are tempting me away from my duties," he teased, setting her a short distance from him. After dropping a softer kiss on her lips, Fane stepped away to pull his phone from his pocket. Quickly, he reviewed her schedule.

"I'll review the report this morning to be ready for my meeting. Then, can you document some notes for me when I return? I'd like to review any modifications or suggestions," she asked.

"You got it, boss." Walking out of the door, he left it open so there was no barrier between them.

Elaine immersed herself in the report. She searched for any shred of doubt or possible mistakes. Finding none, she checked again.

"Boss, you'll need to head to Easton's office to make it there on time."

"Crap! Time escaped me. Thanks!"

Grabbing the hard copy and her computer, Elaine dashed to her boss's office. "Let's get busy, Easton." Piper closed the door when Easton nodded at her and sealed the two in privacy.

* * *

"They still working?" Fane asked three hours later, after he'd followed his boss's path.

"I just ordered them lunch. They're deep into plans for how to present Elaine's report to the shareholders," Piper replied.

"And the survey?" Fane probed.

"I can't say anything specific, but I talked to Sharon this morning prior to searching through her very efficient files for the name of the surveyor Easton trusts."

"That's my girl. She was right."

"Your girl, huh?"

"That seems to be going around, doesn't it?" he asked in return.

"Everyone has secrets here," Piper answered with a knowing smile.

"And you love it here as much as I do," Fane countered.

"I do."

"I'll go attack the files in my office. Want to share the secret of Sharon's system?" he asked, looking over the top of his glasses at her.

"It's all very simple. Just remember where you are and you'll know," Piper shared.

"Edgewater Industries?"

"No, Fane. ABC Towers."

"Amazing. Alphabetical is my system, too. I'm off to sing that silly song to myself—way too many times."

"Bye, Fane. Come up and check on her when you want. Or I could send you a message from time to time?"

"Please message me. Thanks for ordering them lunch."

"You're welcome."

Fane turned and navigated the path back to Elaine's office. He'd use the time as efficiently as possible to get everything put together. Sometimes things had to get messy before they could improve. Pulling all the files from the two four-drawer filing cabinets, he made piles on the floor in organized chaos.

Three hours later, his back ached with leaning over four gazillion times, but he was making headway. He'd put one file cabinet in order. More important, Fane had created a definite plan for the next. The number of duplicate files had been astonishing and incredibly confusing. He'd discarded a huge number of papers in an empty box he'd grabbed from the staff room.

"What the hell happened?"

He turned to face Elaine, standing horrified in the doorway. Fane watched her walk over to pick up a file from his discard stack next to the overflowing trashcan. "Hi, boss. Had a snowball fight with the file cabinet and it won. You wouldn't believe the number of…"

"Fane, this information is classified. It can't just go in the dumpster."

"I'm back, Fane. I finally got that last load wrangled away. What do you want me to take next?"

"Thanks, Colby. You're earning your money today. I think that's the last of the duplicate files there in that box," Fane said, pointing to the box at Elaine's feet. He gently took the file from her hands and put it back on the stack.

"No way!" Elaine spread her arms and positioned herself as the guard to the sensitive information.

"Go get the rest of anything you took from this office and bring it back immediately," she demanded of the employee with the wheeled cart.

"Ma'am, I can't do that…"

"You will figure out a way," Elaine interrupted him coldly.

"Elaine, you don't understand," Fane tried to explain.

"I understand your job is in jeopardy."

Elaine turned back to the man in uniform. "Go get those files. Now!"

"Colby works in the shredding department," Fane said quickly, before she could say anything else. "He will take these also to shred if you will allow him. Everything is being destroyed per company policy."

Elaine's mouth closed with a snap. She stepped away from the papers with a shake of her head. Fane watched her as Colby picked up the papers and stowed them securely on his cart.

"Thank you, Colby. I appreciate you making a field trip to come pick these up. My fault that I hadn't shared my plans with Ms. Rivers. She's been in a meeting all day with Mr. Edgewater. If we're lucky, they came up with some spectacular plans to boost our profit sharing this year."

"No problem, Fane. I'm always glad to return a favor." He pushed the heavy cart through the door and disappeared.

"I have work to do," Elaine pushed through gritted teeth. She turned and walked into her office, closing the door behind her, leaving Fane staring at the wooden barrier.

Walking forward, he paused by the door to listen. A squeak of her office chair, the sigh of the leather chair as Elaine sat down, and a soft sob drifted to his ears. Fane twisted the door handle to find it locked. She really was being naughty.

After locking the outer door, Fane grabbed a paperclip from his desk and uncurled it. With a quick flick of his wrist, he opened the door and walked in quietly. Laney lay draped over her computer, crying. Fane closed and locked the door behind him and walked across the floor to draw her chair back.

Her tearstained face brought out his protective instincts with a roar. Fane chose to console her first. Punishment would come later.

"Go away."

"Nope." Fane scooped her wriggling body out of her chair and pinned her arms to her sides. Controlling her easily, he sat down in her place and held her against him. Slowly, he felt her rigidity ebb from her body, until her head rested in the hollow of his throat.

Releasing her arms, he rubbed the length of her spine. "It's okay, Laney. Daddy's got you."

"You're going to run so far away from me. I screw up everything in my personal life. It's just easier to be alone," she bemoaned.

"That's not an option for you now."

Silence answered him. Fane knew she was thinking so hard he imagined he could feel the vibrations emanating from her brain. He rocked her slowly back and forth, allowing her to take her time.

"You're not leaving? Going to work for someone else?"

"The only person I want to work with is you—when you listen and don't jump to conclusions."

"I was awful. It's not a good excuse, but I've had so many assistants, I never know. And that folder held critical information."

"So critical that there were three copies of it. Each a bit different from the rest. My eyes are going to bleed if I find another copy squirreled away somewhere."

"That's not safe." She peeked up at him.

"I don't think anyone could find anything in the mishmash of files in there. They just made a new copy with whatever they could find when you requested it. While you were in your meeting, I pulled everything out and started organizing. The mess you see in there is important stuff that will go back in the file cabinet. Colby took away all the outdated and duplicated information. He was great to bump us up in the schedule for shredding."

"What favor did he owe you?"

"I showed his son a few magic tricks and did a show for his birthday party. I rock a top hat."

"You do magic?"

"Every day."

"I messed up so bad."

"You didn't listen. You jumped to the wrong conclusion."

"Trust," she whispered, remembering that word from the list they'd created last night.

"You've earned your first consequence. I won't punish you here. I have about an hour of work to do. You said earlier you wanted to make some notes about your meeting with Easton. We'll leave when we're ready and take care of your behavior when we get home."

"You still want me to come to your house?" she asked, looking at him with wide eyes.

"Little girls make mistakes. Their Daddies punish them, and everything disappears. I'm not going to walk away from you, Laney."

Fane boosted her up from his lap. "Get your notes done and then we'll go."

CHAPTER 9

"This is nice," Laney complimented, using the manners her mom had instilled in her at a young age. She looked around the casually comfortable home curiously.

It looked like Fane. It was clean, but not fussy or rigid with everything in a regulated spot. A big fluffy blanket draped over the couch, inviting her to come curl up. He'd piled puzzles and games on the kitchen table. There were magnetic letters on the refrigerator spelling out phrases like Play More and Junk Food Alert.

She considered Fane's hard physique. He didn't look like he lived on snacks or fast food.

"I'd love to know what's going on in your mind, Little girl," Fane commented, wrapping an arm around her waist.

"Oh, nothing," she assured him quickly. "I was just thinking, this house looks like you."

"I'll take that as a compliment." He turned her toward him and cradled her cheek in one palm. "This is a safe place, Laney. You don't have to follow the same social rules as you do in the office. Here you can be yourself."

Laney nodded as her mind whirled, trying to process his words.

Fane added, "Let me give you the grand tour."

Fane waved a hand around the large, open area. "This is the great room and kitchen area. The laundry room is just off the kitchen. Let's go down this hallway. There are three bedrooms: the master, the guest room, and your nursery."

"My nursery?"

"The nursery I created over the last couple of years for my Little girl. I tailored it to you when I found you. So, yeah—it's your nursery."

A thrill zinged through her. Fane was so sure she was his. She liked it.

"We'll go there last. Here's the guest room." He opened a door to reveal a comfortable bedroom in tones of gold and brown.

"Pretty."

"Thanks. I don't have guests very often, but I want them to sleep well and enjoy their time here. Next is the master bedroom," he said before opening that door.

An immense bed dominated the center of the room. Here, the colors were shades of blue and brown. It looked masculine, but welcoming. Not dark, but the light was toned down inside as if he slept better without streaming light to disturb him.

"There's an enormous bathroom through there with a super large tub. I had to upgrade the water heater to have enough hot water to fill it when I moved in, but now you can be toasty warm inside."

"I like to soak in the bathtub," she smiled.

"Would you like to see the nursery now?" he asked, studying her face.

She nodded, unable to talk. Torn between wanting to see it and fear that she'd make a fool of herself, Laney didn't know how to react.

Fane led her back down the hall. He pushed open the door and guided her inside. "Tell me if there's anything you'd like to change. I want you to be happy here."

Looking around in amazement, Laney walked into the center of the room. At the end of the room, a twin bed with a mound of pillows and fluffy bedding sat with a guard rail up on one side while the other side lowered to invite her to jump inside. An elaborate dream catcher in brilliant gemstone colors decorated the wall above the head of the bed.

On the right stretched a large closet with accordion doors. One was partially open to reveal a few garments hanging inside.

"Someone already lives here?" she asked.

"No, Laney. I picked up a few things for you. I wanted you to be comfortable. There's another set of yoga clothes and some play clothes."

"Oh!" she said softly, feeling ridiculous for having jumped to a negative conclusion.

"Ask any questions that pop into your mind. I hope I'll have the right answer that puts your mind at ease. I've worked for Edgewater Industries for three years and lived here for two. I started putting together the nursery when I discovered my side of our connection about sixteen months ago."

"Really? You've waited to meet me for that long?"

"It was hard. But I needed to be able to step into your admin's role. I want to support you at work as much as I take care of you at home."

"You've been very focused."

"I like to enjoy life, but I am dead serious about things that are important to me. You are at the top of that list, Laney. I think it's time for us to talk about your behavior this afternoon."

"I shouldn't have jumped to conclusions. Asking a few questions would have easily set my mind at ease," she said quickly.

"Yes. I'm glad you've already figured out a better way to deal with concerns. That will eliminate your time in your thinking corner this time." Fane pointed to an undecorated corner next to the closet.

"Thinking corner?"

"All Littles need time to process through negative behavior. I'll never send you to the corner to stand. I'll send you there to think. When you've had time to cool down and come up with a better way to handle problems, you can come out."

"So, everything's okay now?" she asked with a smile.

"Not quite. Now, I need to address your behavior. You violated a key component to our guidelines."

"I didn't trust you, but that takes time," she said quickly to excuse her behavior.

"Trust will build," he agreed before adding, "Did you even consider perhaps I had made the right decision, or did you jump to the conclusion that I'd majorly screwed up?"

"Well… Okay, I figured you were like everyone else. I'm not used to relying on anyone," Laney tried to explain. Even to her ears, the excuse sounded lame.

"It's time to change that."

Fane reached around her and unfastened the waistband of her skirt. When she clutched the front to keep it from dropping, he met her gaze. "Laney, it's time to trust your Daddy. How badly do you feel about judging me negatively this afternoon?"

"Really bad."

"Then let's wipe away that guilt. Let it go."

"Are you going to spank me?"

"Yes."

"I don't want a spanking," she whispered, feeling tears already gathering in her eyes. Laney blinked furiously, trying to ward them off.

"I know."

He held her gaze steadily until, finally, she released her hold on the crisp material. When he nodded his approval, she relaxed a fraction. Fane hooked his fingers into the sides of her panties and knelt in front of her to pull them down to her ankles.

Half dressed in front of him, Laney suddenly felt very Little. Knowing she shouldn't hide from his view, she clasped her fingers behind her. "Daddy?"

"You're being a very good Little girl, Laney. Daddy's proud of you. Step out of your shoes," he instructed, running his hand down the outside of one calf. When she lifted her foot, he removed the pump and eased her panties off on that side. Quickly, he repeated his attention to her other leg.

Fane smoothly rose to his feet and kissed her forehead. "Come lie over my lap, Laney."

Without waiting for her answer, he walked a short distance to a large, armless chair. Fane sat down and held up one hand for her to join him.

It was up to her. *Can I do this?*

Laney forced herself to take one baby step forward and then another. His gaze held hers, silently encouraging her to accept her correction. Finally, she reached him. Swallowing hard against the lump in her throat, she leaned across his lap as he helped her move into position. One of his hands pressed firmly into the small of her back as the other rubbed over her exposed skin.

Before she could take a breath, he swatted her bare bottom sharply. The sound rang out in the silent room and the sting made her rear up to look back at him.

"That hurt!"

Fane lifted his hand and dropped it again on a new spot as he calmly instructed, "Drop your fingertips to the carpet, Little girl."

His restraining hand shifted further up Laney's spine to move her back into the correct position. The other continued to pepper her bottom with stinging swats. Tears welled in her eyes as her skin heated.

"Daddy, no!" she pleaded.

"You're taking your punishment very well, Laney. I'm proud of you."

"Nooo!" she wailed, wiggling to scoot off his lap, but Fane held her in place.

"Your spanking will stop when you accept the correction," he said gently.

"Accept?" she repeated, trying to figure out what that meant. Tears streamed from her eyes to soak into the carpet below her.

Finally, she collapsed over his lap, unable to think of anything but the fire building in her skin. "I'm sorry!" she sobbed. "I'm sorry!"

Immediately, his hand switched from spanking her to rubbing the punished flesh. "That's my girl," he praised.

Slowly, he lifted her to sit on his lap. Laney hissed as her fiery skin touched the fine wool of his slacks. She collapsed against his chest, crying harder than she had in years.

"You're okay, Laney. Everything is wiped away now. Just let me hold you," Fane crooned to her as he rocked her in his arms.

Laney buried her head against his dress shirt, tangling her fingers in the material. Her sobs eased, and she rubbed her cheeks over his shirt to wipe away the moisture from her face.

"Did you just blow your nose on Daddy?" he teased.

"No," she denied, horrified. Sitting up, she met his laughing eyes. He wasn't mad at her. Suddenly, Laney's guilt at jumping to the negative conclusion in the office disappeared.

Flinging her arms around his neck, Laney hugged her Daddy close.

"Feel better?" he asked.

"Yes, Daddy. All but my butt."

"A punished bottom will remind you to think twice. You'll probably have red cheeks under your skirts for a while."

"No. I've learned my lesson."

Laney stared at him when he chuckled. She was determined to be a good girl to prove him wrong.

CHAPTER 10

"Eat two bites more," Fane encouraged as they sat at the kitchen island. Too wound up, she hadn't eaten much of her dinner.

"I'm done. Thank you. It was delicious," she complimented as she pulled away the napkin that he'd tucked into the neck of her new T-shirt. Her breasts bobbled. It felt weird not to be wearing a bra, but he'd assured her she didn't need it here.

"Two more bites," he repeated, drawing her back out of her thoughts before giving her another option. "Or you can drink a bottle if you'd prefer."

"A bottle?" she echoed in surprise.

"I think that's a good idea, too. Let me get these dishes put away and I'll fix you Daddy's special concoction."

Laney stared at him as he moved to the other side of the island to open the dishwasher. Her memory flashed back to that list. She'd agreed to try different things. Squirming on her sore bottom, Laney knew she didn't want any more punishments.

"What's your favorite reptile?" he asked, drawing her attention back to him.

"That's a weird question."

"It's strange question time. I'll ask one and you ask the next. So, reptile?"

"I like iguanas. I saw a video clip of one falling out of a tree when the temperature dropped too low. They're like me. I don't like cold, either."

"I'll remember to put a blanket around you so you don't fall out. Your turn."

"What's the thing you like least about being my admin?"

"That's not a weird question. I'll make you go again, but first let me answer. I don't like not being able to do more to take the pressure of your job off your shoulders."

"You don't have to worry about that. I actually thrive on the daily challenges," she answered with a smile.

"I'm glad you enjoy your job. Now, weird question," he directed, sending her a serious look.

"What do you put on your peanut butter sandwiches?"

"Dill pickles."

"Pickles? Yuck!" she exclaimed, scrunching her nose in disgust.

"Have you tried it?" Fane asked with an arched eyebrow.

"Well, no. But that's an awful combination," Laney protested.

"We'll try it tomorrow."

"Not me!"

"More for me then," he answered, closing the dishwasher.

Laney watched him open a cabinet and pull out a large plastic container that rattled as he moved it. When he opened it, she stretched taller to see inside. Glass bottles and other bits filled the bin. He selected a smaller bottle with a matching nipple and ring.

Fane pulled a large cylinder from a drawer in the cabinet and opened it. After scooping a portion of the powder into the measuring cup inside, he dumped it into the bottle. A few shakes of a couple of spice containers and a small tilt of a brown bottle followed before he added milk to fill it almost to the top.

"This is your concoction?"

"Just wait. Super yummy." He screwed a flat lid on the bottle and shook it vigorously.

Dancing around the island as he mixed it up, Fane sang in his beautiful baritone, "Shake, shake, shake."

When he looked at her expectantly and pointed a hand her way, she sang it back to him, "Shake, shake, shake!"

"Make it delicious," he finished. "Voila!"

Fane replaced the flat lid with the nipple threaded through the ring. He held it to his mouth and sucked experimentally. "Perfect in every way."

She couldn't help but laugh at his complete faith in himself. "Of course it is!"

Laney watched him round the island to stand next to her. When he offered her his free hand, she took it and let her Daddy help her from the counter stool. Following him to the couch, she sank down into the soft leather seat next to him as he tugged her gently into place. Soon, she lay across his lap with her shoulders supported by a cushion.

"Try this," he suggested, brushing the nipple lightly over her lips.

"Daddy..." Laney's statement stopped as he fit the rubbery tip into her mouth as she spoke.

"Drink."

Tentatively, she sucked. Sweet liquid filled her mouth. It tasted like a melted milkshake with a hint of cinnamon and vanilla.

"Mmm!" she murmured as she drew on it again.

"Yummy, isn't it?" Fane stroked his fingers through her hair as he held the bottle at precisely the right angle for her to drink deeply.

"My Little girl is so precious."

Staring at him, she drank happily. His gaze never left her as the delicious mixture flowed into her mouth. His love for Laney shone in his eyes. It was as if there was no one else in the world—just her Daddy and her. She wiggled, getting a bit more comfortable in his arms. Laney enjoyed having this quiet time together.

Too soon, the bottle was empty. Fane lifted her to lean against his chest. He rocked her slowly until she struggled to keep her eyes open. Soon, she gave up that battle and closed her eyes.

Something warm and strong supported her as she stumbled, more than half asleep, across the carpet. Following his directions, she used the potty, sighing in delight as her still warm bottom met the cool seat. She wrinkled her nose in dislike at the low chuckle that followed but braced her shoulder against him as he whisked her shorts, panties, and socks off.

"I can do it," she protested as he wiped between her legs.

"You're too Little, baby girl. Daddy will help."

That made perfect sense to her sleepy mind. "Okay," she mumbled, and felt him press a kiss on her lips.

When her teeth were brushed in the dimly lit room, he guided her to the enormous bed. After taking off her shirt, he drew the bedclothes back. "Time for bed, Little girl."

Climbing into the crisp sheets when his hand cupped her bare cheeks to urge her into bed, Laney settled on her side facing the center of the bed. Her Daddy tucked her knees up and held them in place as he stroked the seam of her pussy before caressing her red bottom.

"I'll be good," she mumbled.

"I'll watch to catch you being good. Daddy wants to reward you, too. Sleep now."

"You come sleep now," she whispered as she nestled into the soft pillow.

"Soon."

* * *

LANEY WOKE the next morning cuddled against his warmth. Her Daddy's arm was thrown over her body, resting just under her breasts and pinning her in place. Glancing at the clock, she noted the early time and relaxed. She didn't need to get up yet.

That arm across her moved, and Fane cupped her breast. His fingers smoothed over the soft mound and rolled her nipple deliciously. She squirmed in response, wanting more of his sleepy caresses.

"Who's this wiggle worm in my bed?" he asked, raising his head to meet her gaze. "It's not a worm. It's a Laney."

"Hi, Daddy," she grinned at his silliness.

He leaned over her to press a kiss to her lips. "Mmm, more!" he demanded, pulling her to his chest as he rolled to his side. His mouth teased and tempted hers with soft kisses. When she rested fully against him, Fane deepened the kiss as he pressed her pelvis to his with a firm hand on her lower back.

His thick cock thrust stiffly into the curve of her tummy. She moved tentatively against him. In response, Fane's hand drifted over her sore bottom to lift her top leg over his hip. Holding her in place, he nestled his shaft against her intimately. He rocked against her, gliding intimately into her blossoming wetness.

"Fane?" she whispered when his mouth lifted from hers. She wasn't sure what she was asking.

"It's okay, Little girl. I've got you," he reassured her, continuing his strokes against her body. "Are you ready for Daddy to make you his completely?"

"Please!"

He threaded his fingers through her hair and brought her lips back to his. Deepening the kiss, he explored the inside of her mouth. Fane tangled his tongue with hers, tempting her to respond completely and eagerly.

"No!" she protested when he lifted his lips from hers.

"Shh!" he soothed as he pressed kisses and nibbled against the sensitive skin of her neck.

She squirmed against him as his teeth closed over that spot at the curve of her shoulder. Her movements pressed her pussy against his steely shaft, bringing a gasp to her lips. Unable to stop herself, Laney repeated the motion, thrilled at the sensations.

Fane's caresses made her lean back slightly as he trailed scorching kisses over her collarbones and lower. His path took him so close to her breast. Laney breathed deeply, lifting herself toward his mouth. When his fiery mouth closed over one beaded nipple, she curled her nails into his shoulders as she arched her back.

Slowly, he explored her body as he continued the rocking motion that was driving her arousal higher and higher. Fane bit that sensitive peak and rolled it between his teeth, giving her a hint of pain that thrilled her.

Laney explored his body with her hands. Stroking his skin stretched over hard muscles, she tugged at the silky, dark hair sprinkled over his chest. Daringly, she trailed her fingertips down the narrowing trail to his pelvis.

Just as her fingers brushed the broad head of his cock, Fane rolled away from her, bringing a cry to her lips. "No!" she wailed.

"Soon, Laney. I need to protect you," he reassured her, rolling back to press an urgent kiss to her lips before leaning away to rustle in the nightstand drawer. Withdrawing a box, he ripped it open using his teeth. He returned with a string of condoms before tearing one free.

"Open this," he requested as he tucked the others under the pillow.

Bumbling with the wrapper, she got it open, pulling out the brightly colored protective sheath as Fane shifted onto his back. With practiced ease Laney didn't want to consider, he rolled the condom over his shaft.

Unable to stop herself, she blurted, "It glows in the dark!"

"Supposedly tastes like passion fruit."

Instinctively, she leaned forward to lick it. He stopped her by encircling her waist with his hands to move her to straddle him.

"You can taste next time. I need to be inside you now."

Laney nodded eagerly and bounced against him experimentally, bringing a groan to both their lips.

"Up now," he directed, boosting her up by her waist. With Laney poised over him on her knees, Fane moved one hand to place his cock at her entrance.

"Slowly, Laney," he urged, coaxing her to lower herself.

Licking her lips subconsciously, Laney sank down slowly, feeling his thick shaft entering her. Her hands dropped to his chest as he filled her, needing to tether herself to his strength. She'd never been with anyone as endowed as Fane. When her pelvis met his, she met his gaze triumphantly.

"Good girl," he praised, running his hands over her shoulders. He lifted his hips slightly to press deeper inside her.

"Ooh!" she gasped, feeling him press again. Those sensitive spots inside her flared into life. Her fingernails bit into his shoulders as he moved again. Tentatively, she rose on her knees a small amount and lowered herself again.

"Mmm!" she moaned.

"Just wait, Laney." His hands slid from her waist, up her sensitive sides, to cup her breasts. Fane's slightly rough thumbs brushed over her tightened peaks, making her shiver in reaction.

Her squirms increased the fire building inside her. Laney didn't ever remember wanting anyone this much. She already knew the pleasure that he could bring her. With growing speed, she moved over him. His hips rising to meet her downward strokes ended with a twist that brought a gasp of delight to her lips. He watched her carefully, adjusting his movements to drive her crazy.

Laney lost track of time as they ground their bodies together. Perspiration gathered on their skin, allowing their hands to glide over each other. She pressed kisses over his face and chest, savoring his taste and scent. A climax crashed over her without warning.

"Daddy!" she screamed into the space as his hands tightened around her waist as he increased his thrusts. His orgasm sparked hers to reignite as he filled the condom within her.

As their bodies calmed, she collapsed over him, feeling his arms surround her to erase any space between them. Laney pressed a kiss to his neck as she settled against him.

"I didn't know sex could be that good," she whispered.

"Our lovemaking will only get better," he promised.

"Lovemaking?" she repeated, catching his subtle correction.

"Yes, Little girl." He hugged her close before patting her sore bottom. "Now, unfortunately, one high-powered executive needs to shower and go to work."

"Oh, crap!" she panicked, looking at the clock.

"We have time. I'll claim more cuddle time later," he stated, helping her shift off him before scrambling off the bed.

CHAPTER 11

She arrived at the office with a scant number of minutes left before the meeting with the board. After grabbing her files, Elaine raced to Easton's office to greet all the attendees and settle into her place at the table. As the meeting began, she took a deep breath and smiled. The faint soreness of her bottom, combined with the mirroring sensation from his possession between her legs, distracted her from the stress of the gathering. The shortness of time that morning had distracted her completely.

When her time came to review the report she'd created, Elaine could tell her presentation resonated with the board. When she revealed the results of the survey they had on record and the second one Fane had expedited, everyone had leaned in to read the updated results.

"So, there is a possibility of expansion. This is the extra space we need to expand the campus to meet this latest goal Easton has envisioned for Edgewater Industries," she shared proudly.

A flurry of questions came from the board members. Easton and Elaine had prepared thoroughly. Piper supported their recommendations with freshly printed documents and spreadsheets as well as notepads and pens for jotting thoughts and questions. It appeared they had thought of everything. She couldn't wait to get back to Fane to share with him the group's reactions.

At the lunch break, she felt a hand on her shoulder as a chair pulled up behind her. "I hear you're killing them. Take these painkillers to ward off the headache you're getting. Piper tells me you've rubbed your temples a couple of times. No, no one else has noticed," Fane assured her as he slipped her two tablets under the table.

"Sign this paper for me. They all will think I needed your very valuable signature," he said softly, as their heads bent together.

"That's all I needed, Ms. Rivers. Sorry to disturb your lunch," he apologized in a louder voice before adding more quietly, "Eat. You need fuel."

"Thanks, Fane," she smiled at him, realizing that just seeing his handsome face bolstered her as much as it warded off the approaching headache. Elaine tried to school her features professionally as she turned back to answer a question from the board member sitting next to her as he headed for the door. Scanning the room as he left, she took a covert glance at his muscular butt before he disappeared through the conference room door.

Damn, her Daddy was fine.

By the end of the day, Elaine was exhausted, despite Easton's infectious elation. They had done it. She thanked Piper for all her work and gathered her notes to take back to her office. Easton caught her at the door.

"Elaine, you saved the day today, paving the way for Edgewater Industries to take a step past our competitors. Thank you for your hard work on this. Piper tells me you'd like to talk to me about changing your administrative assistant again."

"No need, Easton. Fane is turning out to be exactly what I needed in my office. We're becoming quite a team."

"I'm glad to hear that. You've been working solo for too long. We all need someone who has our backs," Easton said meaningfully as he glanced at Piper, accepting compliments from the last lingering board member.

"He's definitely not who I envisioned as my assistant, but I can't imagine working without him. He's the one who wrangled the mess my rotating temporary help had left to find that report we needed."

"Then I owe him my thanks as well. Have him come see me tomorrow morning at nine. I'd like to talk to him."

"You're not going to try and steal Fane away, are you?" Elaine asked directly.

"Not a chance. Sharon was right in selecting Piper to fill her position."

"I'm concerned about Sharon," Elaine confessed. "I saw her at yoga the other night, but she had to leave early."

"I'm worried about her as well. Her life is very difficult these days and it won't get any easier, I'm afraid."

The two stood quietly, thinking for a few seconds before Easton ordered, "We'll worry about that later. For tonight, go celebrate our accomplishments from today. We'll talk next week about your yearly bonus. You definitely earned your pay today."

He patted her on the arm before moving away to save Piper from Mr. Thompson's stories about back when Edgewater Industries began. Elaine liked the way his hand nestled in the small of her back. Their closeness reminded her of Fane, and she hurried from the room before she could get drawn into the conversation as well. That's why Easton earned the huge bucks. He was always the last to leave.

"Oh!" She gasped at finding Fane leaning against the door as she exited.

"Time to go, Ms. Rivers. You have that important meeting you ordered me to help you remember. There's just enough time to get you to your transportation," Fane announced as they approached the elevator.

In moments, he whisked her outside and into a waiting car. Urging her over, Fane slid in next to her. He leaned forward to speak quietly to the driver.

"Where are we going?" Laney asked.

"Dinner first and then a treat," he explained as the car threaded its way through the rush hour traffic downtown.

"Really? What are we doing?"

"You'll have to wait to see," Fane answered mysteriously as he held out his hand for hers.

"I don't know if I like surprises," Laney answered, wrinkling her nose.

"You'll like this one."

With a sniff of doubt, she settled back against him to watch the cars and people bustling around. Soon, the car pulled up at the front entrance of a popular fondue restaurant. She'd always wanted to try it but… it was designed for more than one diner.

"Come on, Laney girl. Gooey cheese is waiting," he urged as he slid from the back seat.

"And chocolate?" she said, scooting out behind him.

"Definitely. I'm not leaving before dessert." With a wink, he leaned forward to update the driver on their plans.

With a squeeze of her hand as he stood again by her side, Fane asked, "Ready?"

Laney nodded. She was so excited. Walking in next to him, she looked around the dimly lit restaurant at all the private dining tables, each featuring the traditional heat source in the center. At their reserved table, she slid into the bench seat and cuddled close to him as Fane joined her on that side. His hand covered her bouncing knee as he ordered a glass of white wine for each of them.

"I think we need to celebrate, don't you?" he asked after the server left.

"It all went so well," Laney enthused. "Easton and I knew how they'd respond when given the chance to expand. It wouldn't have been possible if we hadn't proven that survey wrong."

"It's a good thing we found it," Fane smiled fondly at her before leaning in to kiss her lightly.

"Here we go, folks," the waitress interrupted them, setting their glasses on the table. "What would you like tonight? The traditional Swiss fondue?"

"And chocolate," Laney added quickly.

"There are three kinds of chocolate fondue on our menu: traditional milk chocolate, dark chocolate, or chocolate with a hint of Irish cream."

"Laney? Do you have a preference?"

"Milk chocolate with plenty of marshmallows, please," she requested.

"You've been here before," the server answered with a smile.

"No. I've just wanted to come for a long time," Laney answered.

"I'm glad you've made it here. You'll have to return and try the others. They're all good. I'm going to make a note to bring extra brownie pieces, too. Those are my favorites," the waitress said with a smile before she left.

"This is so much fun. Thank you for bringing me here. How did you think of it?" Laney asked.

"I saw the menu printed off in your apartment and thought it was your favorite. Now, I'm even happier to be here with you." Fane lifted his wineglass to clink against hers.

Leaning forward, he whispered, "Everyone else sees the grownup with her glass of wine, while I know the Little girl who lurks inside."

She beamed at him and took a sip of the crisp beverage. Relaxing against the leather seat, Laney studied Fane's face. How had it been only a few days since he'd come into her life? Dropping her eyes to his powerful forearms, she traced one of the colorful tattoos decorating his skin. She should never have judged this book by its cover.

"I think I'll need a new one," he murmured.

"Really?"

"I'll come up with a design and let you know. I've been saving the perfect place for it," Fane said, patting his chest over his heart.

Laney started to tear up, but blinked them away as the server wheeled her cart up to the table to begin the ritual of crafting the first molten concoction. When she left the table brimming with goodies to dip inside, Laney already had a forked skewer in her hand.

"Dig in, Daddy," she urged Fane before realizing what she'd said. Laney looked around to see if anyone was paying attention. To her relief, no one seemed remotely interested in their conversation.

Grinning, she dipped a potato into the mixture and popped it into her mouth. Laney wiggled happily, forgetting about her sore bottom, before freezing in place. Fane's laughter made her wave her fork in a mock threat that made his eyes glitter even more with delight.

By the time the cheese had disappeared, Laney had shared everything from the meeting. "It couldn't have gone more perfectly," she summed up.

"I'm glad to hear that," the pert server quipped.

"Oh, I was talking about a meeting," Laney began before laughing as the waitress did.

"Ready for chocolate?"

"Bring it on!" Fane encouraged, sitting back to pat his flat belly. "I have room for exactly three marshmallows and two brownies left."

"You're going to need more than that," the server warned as she cleared the table of the savory course.

A half hour later, Fane ushered a chocolate- and marshmallow-filled Laney back into the car. "Stop two, please," he instructed the driver.

"Where are we going?" Laney asked, trying to guess as they drove through the city.

"You'll know soon," he promised.

"I could tickle it out of you," she threatened, scooting close to him.

"I do not recommend that. I ate way more than I should have."

The car came to a stop, preventing her from commenting on Fane's chocolate gluttony. It had been a good thing they had extra marshmallows and brownies.

"What? You got us tickets?"

"I did. Ready to go watch some singing and dancing?" Fane asked before opening the door.

Laney bounced in place next to him on the sidewalk as he closed the door. She loved musicals. Reading the sparkling reviews of this presentation, she'd almost bought one ticket to the play, but the thought of driving downtown, parking, and walking back to her car alone had deterred her.

"How did you know?" she whispered when they sat in the perfect seats—not too close and not too far from the stage.

"I didn't. I took a gamble. Thank goodness you love the theater as much as I do. My mom always had season tickets for the family. She was determined to raise my sisters and me as cultured heathens. My dad died too early, so I accompanied her for years until she remarried about five years ago. I've missed it. I'm glad to have someone to enjoy it with."

"I'd love to come with you. There's a great one next month," she suggested. "It's kind of for kids, but I'd like to see it."

"Then I'll get us some tickets. I'll look into when season tickets reopen," he commented easily as he opened his program to scan the actors. When she didn't answer, he looked over to meet her gaze.

"Are you planning for us to be together for a while?" she asked, trying to keep herself from looking too hopeful.

"I'm never letting you go, Little girl. Shh! It's starting." He reached his arm around the back of her seat to hold her close.

"I hear this is the best part," Fane whispered with his lips pressed to her ear to avoid disturbing the crowd as everyone fell silent.

Laney couldn't have chosen a favorite part. The show was a total delight. Drowsing on his shoulder on the way back to the Edgewater campus later than she normally stayed up, Laney knew she'd have loved spending time with Fane anywhere.

CHAPTER 12

In the aftermath of the big meeting and the fun evening out leading to less than her desired amount of sleep, Elaine found herself snapping at everyone the next day. She told herself she wasn't being unpleasant, but just expecting that everyone else would put in one hundred percent as she always did. That didn't ring quite true even to her, but Laney couldn't pull herself out of the negative rut.

Walking out of her office to find Fane gone, Elaine checked his schedule. She'd forgotten about his meeting with Easton at nine. Stomping back into her office, she tried to bury herself in work but kept looking through their connecting door to see if he'd returned. Finally, she heard the squeak of Fane's chair.

Elaine rushed into the outer office. "What did he want?"

"I'm glad to be back. Thank you, Elaine, for welcoming me," Fane corrected her greeting.

"Did he want to move you to a different position?" she probed, dismissing his words with a wave of her hand.

"He did not. Easton asked if I'd be willing to represent the administrative assistants as he meets with staff member groups. We talked about training needs."

"Nothing personal?" she interrogated.

"Do you want to rethink that tone?" Fane asked with narrowed eyes at her demanding approach.

"Fine. Keep secrets. I'm going back to work. I'd suggest you do the same." Elaine turned on her heels and stomped back into her office. When Fane didn't follow her, she forced herself to concentrate on the report in front of her from the accounting division.

Her bad mood continued through the morning and didn't improve when he insisted she accompany him to get something for lunch.

"How hard is it to get a sandwich right?" she complained to the employee in the cafeteria. "I hate mayonnaise. You'll have to make it again."

"Yes, ma'am," the young woman said as she picked up the plate Laney had shoved toward the edge of the table. "My apologies."

"It's fine, Arielle. I'll eat that one and Ms. Rivers can have mine. It's made with mustard." Fane intercepted the plate and dismissed the new employee with a kind smile.

"If you're sure?" Arielle asked before escaping quickly at Fane's nod.

"You don't have to eat that. It has tomatoes on it. You just said you don't like tomatoes," Elaine complained.

"I have a perfect solution." Fane lifted the top piece of bread and removed the tomato. He grabbed the mustard on the table and squeezed a healthy portion on top of the mayo.

"She would have remade it. That's her job," Elaine commented as she picked up the sandwich in front of her. "Ugh. I forgot you ordered turkey." Raising her hand, she waved, trying to get a server's attention.

Fane captured her hand and pressed it to the table. "Let's just go back to the office. I'll run out and get you something else to eat."

"You're right. It will take forever to get anything here. They are so slow. I'll just eat this. It's not like I hate turkey." Elaine took another bite as she looked speculatively around.

"Easton should update the food model here on campus. I bet we could attract a couple of name-brand companies to come in and set up shops."

"All these employees would lose their jobs, Laney."

"Elaine." She corrected him without seeming to notice. "They could probably get another job with the restaurants that open here."

"I don't think the employees would appreciate that change. Look over there. The secretarial pool is having a bridal shower for one of the long-time admins. Two of the guests are employees in this department. I bet they scheduled it in the cafeteria so they could attend on their lunch break. These people are part of the Edgewater family."

"Hmm. I guess." Elaine took another bite and dropped the sandwich on the plate. "Ugh. I'm not hungry, I guess. I'm going back to my desk to get some things done."

"Nope." Fane hooked his foot around the leg of her chair to hold her in place. "You need a break from the office."

"I'm not kidding, Fane. I have work to do. Let go of my chair." She knew he wouldn't make a scene here.

Fane shook his head and released her chair. "I'll be up when my break is over," he commented, waving as someone called his name from the celebrating group across the room.

"Go join your friends. Just don't forget we have work to do."

"I will be there in exactly twenty-two minutes."

Shaking her head, Elaine stood and navigated her way through the milling crowd in the busy cafeteria. Her exasperation level visibly increased every time she had to move around a clump of employees paused to socialize. At the door, she stopped to look back. The table she had shared with Fane was empty, and she spotted him pulling out a chair at the party table.

"Harrumph," she thought in disgust.

"Have a good day, Ms. Rivers," a friendly voice called her way.

Elaine waved a hand in that direction without looking as she pushed open the door. Maybe without Fane distracting her, she'd get some work done. That shook her out of her grumpy mood a bit. She knew everyone wasn't acting any differently than they normally did. Her patience had worn dangerously thin. Time to lock herself in her office and avoid everyone.

* * *

"Time to leave for yoga," Fane announced at the door to her inner office.

"I'm not going," she answered without looking up from the computer screen before her.

"The workday's over, boss. Time to go home."

"I've got more to do here. I'll see you in the morning."

"Save your work," he instructed.

"Why?" she asked as she automatically followed his directions. Losing data was everyone's worst nightmare.

"Because you're walking out of this office before I carry you out," he told her softly.

"I'll see you after class, Fane. Stop and get me before you leave," she said absentmindedly as the information she was working on pulled her focus back to the screen.

"What? Don't do that!" Elaine protested as her screen went blank.

"Am I smiling?" he asked. "If not, I'm not joking."

A small voice in the back of her mind registered a warning. Planning to work on her phone, Elaine stood. "Okay. I'll call it a day here."

"Thank you. Now, yoga or do you want to wait at your apartment for me?" Fane asked.

"I'll just go home."

"I'll be there right after class. Pack a bag with several work outfits."

"I'll just see you tomorrow," Elaine countered.

Fane pulled his phone from his pocket and selected a number. "Hi, Angi. Sorry to call at the last minute, but something has come up. Can you teach class tonight?"

He listened carefully, keeping an eye on Laney who shook her head furiously. "Thanks, Angi. I owe you one."

"Okay, let's go. We'll stop at your apartment to pick up an outfit for tomorrow."

"Really, Fane. I'm just going to go home and crash. I'll see you tomorrow."

"I'll walk you to your apartment."

"Not necessary," she corrected him breezily.

"It is for me." He ushered her out of the building and across the green space to B Tower.

"Class tonight?" Knox called across the lobby.

"Angi's covering for me. Something's come up," Fane answered with a neutral expression.

"Ah. Gotcha. I'll see you next week, then," the large man answered.

The ride to her floor in the elevator was silent. Each time she looked at Fane, he was studying her. She couldn't figure out what to say, so she finally just stared at the flooring until she could escape from the small enclosure.

At her door, Elaine turned to Fane. "I'm good now. See you tomorrow." She attempted to dart into her apartment. His hand interrupted that plan.

"Invite me in, Little girl."

"I'll just touch base with you in the office," she answered, trying to maintain her control.

"Invite me in. I will leave if you wish me to after we talk," Fane assured her.

With a heavy sigh, she stepped out of the doorway and allowed him to enter. "Listen, Fane. I'm just tired. I didn't get enough sleep last night and I'm dead on my feet."

Fane didn't comment, just scooped her into his arms and carried Elaine over to the couch. Sitting her across his lap, Fane slipped her shoes off and dropped them to the floor. Without a word, he massaged the insole of one foot, bringing a groan to her lips.

"Fane, you don't need to take care of me. I'll be fine. I've made it on my own for eleven years since I graduated."

"That's exactly right. You've 'made' it," he said, stressing one word deliberately. "There's more to life than just surviving it."

"Yeah, yeah, yeah. I know. You have to have fun. Life's boring without joy. You've told me all that. It works most days, but today I'm just too tired. Today, I'm surviving," she answered with a careless wave of her hand.

"I'm sorry I didn't take better care of you last night."

"What? It was great. I loved the play and dinner out was delicious. I'd always wanted to go there, as you know." She stifled a groan as he switched feet to erase the ache of the day away from the other one.

"Separately, either would have been perfect. I checked into weekend matinees for our season tickets. We can get good seats on Saturday or Sunday afternoon. Then, it won't interfere with your sleep."

"I can stay up late," she protested, clamping her teeth shut to ward off the yawn that threatened.

"Daddies need to learn about the beautiful women who are their Littles. I now know late nights do not go well for Laney."

"I'm just tired. I was too wound up to sleep last night when we got home."

"Too much chocolate as well," he said knowingly.

"That didn't keep me awake. I went right to sleep, but then, I woke up a while later."

"And couldn't go back to sleep?"

"No," she said sadly. "I replayed the musical in my mind and made a plan for the next time we go eat fondue. I also picked out some other restaurants to try."

When he looked at her in concern, she rushed to say, "I got back to sleep around five."

"That was not enough recharging time for you."

"No. I've always gone to bed earlyish."

"Now I know, too. That doesn't, however, excuse your behavior today," he said sternly.

"I was fine."

"You were coldly professional to everyone. Did you notice how people avoided you today?"

"Everyone but you," she snapped, covering her sadness at his observation with an accusation. "I got a lot of work done."

"And missed potential connections with people. How do you feel in here?" He pressed a hand to her chest.

"I'm okay," she bluffed.

"That's a lie." He watched her face until she dropped her gaze away.

"You pushed me away today. Have you decided I'm not the Daddy for you?"

"No," she refuted quickly. "I'm just tired. I want to sleep in my own bed."

"Blueberry and Ballsy are waiting for you in your crib," he reminded her.

"Oh," she said quietly.

She'd forgotten that she'd really be sleeping alone in her apartment. Laney bent her knees up to wrap her hands around her shins. When his arms wrapped around the compact bundle she had pulled herself into, she sat stiffly for several seconds before giving in to the comfort he offered.

"Want to go home to sleep in your nursery?" he asked when she yawned against his chest.

"Please."

"Let's go pack a few clothes for the next couple of days and then we'll go find your stuffies."

With Fane's help, she ended up with shoes, makeup, underwear, and three outfits. She wouldn't need anything else in her nursery. Wearing jeans and a T-shirt, Laney held Fane's hand as he locked her apartment door with her duffle strapped over his body.

Knox was missing from the front desk, reminding Laney that she'd kept Fane from teaching yoga. As they walked quietly to Fane's car, she wondered how she could make up for her actions today. Tiredness clouded her brain, making it impossible for her to problem solve.

Impulsively, she asked, "Can you help me figure out how to erase this day?"

"Wiping it away is impossible. People will remember how you treated them. You can, however, make it better."

"Even you? Could you ever forgive me?"

"Daddies are a special case, Laney. They always see the best in their Littles. That doesn't mean there won't be consequences."

"More spankings?"

"Maybe. We'll decide together tomorrow what will make you feel better."

"I'll decide on no spanking," Laney assured him.

"Let's think about that tomorrow. Slide into your seat and I'll fasten your seatbelt," he urged as he opened the passenger door.

A quick ride to the individual housing section of the campus later, Laney forced herself out of the comfortable bucket seat to follow Fane inside. Going straight to her nursery, she laid her torso on the soft bed to talk to her stuffies.

"I'm sorry that I almost left you here alone. I'm glad you've got each other," she whispered.

Lifting her head when she heard Fane at the door, she admitted, "I'm so tired."

"Bath, bottle, and bed."

"Can't I just go to bed?" she whined, hating the sound of her own voice.

"You'll sleep better if you'll follow my directions. The tub's filling now. Let's get these big girl clothes off," Fane directed, holding out a hand to pull her off the bed.

Laney cooperated, relaxing a bit more as each piece of clothing slid from her body. Soon she was wrapped in a thick robe, and Fane scooped her into his arms to carry her into the master bathroom. Yawning, she rested her cheek against his broad chest.

At the sight of the steaming water, she smiled against his skin. "That looks so good."

Fane helped her sit safely inside the large tub. When she was settled, leaning against the back, he kissed her forehead. "Soak and relax for a minute. Daddy will be right back."

She'd almost fallen asleep in the scant minutes he'd left the room. The click of the glass bottle on the vanity made her blink her eyes. Suddenly, she was very thirsty for the delicious concoction.

When she reached her hands out toward the bottle, Fane promised, "Soon, Laney. Let Daddy get you clean first."

Grumbling, she began to argue but fell silent as he stripped off his shirt and trousers before kneeling by the side of the tub to pick up a bumpy, natural sponge. The soapy strokes of the soft material over her body felt so good, making her already relaxed muscles melt into the warm water. Fane didn't attempt to arouse her in any way, but simply washed her thoroughly.

When her breath caught as he cleaned between her thighs, her Daddy kissed the top of her head before saying, "We'll play later, Laney. I promise."

Soon, he plucked her from the water to stand on the absorbent mat. She wobbled in front of him. Fane dried her skin with a thirsty towel before wrapping her once again in the thick robe to carry her to the nursery. He snagged the bottle on his way from the warm bathroom.

Cradled in his arms, she opened her mouth to suck on the nipple as he brought it to her lips. The yummy mixture filled her mouth as she eagerly drank. It was warm this time and comforting. Heat gathered in her tummy as he rocked her slowly. Both combined to lull her deeply into sleep.

She remembered whispering something important to her Daddy before succumbing to her exhaustion. The last thing she remembered was hearing, "I love you too, Laney."

CHAPTER 13

"Daddy?" Laney called, sitting up in bed. "Daddy? What time is it?" The railings were raised on three sides of the bed, confining her in place. She rattled one experimentally. Solid as a rock.

"Morning, Little girl. You slept well. I was just on my way to wake you up."

"There's no clock in here," she complained, rubbing her eyes sleepily.

"Exactly." Fane lowered the side rail to sit next to her.

At the feel of his warm hand stroking over her back, Laney realized she was naked and instinctively pulled the covers up.

"Never hide from Daddy," Fane corrected, gently tugging them from her hands. "Do you need to potty?"

At his reminder, a sudden urge flashed through Laney's body. She nodded and fumbled with the covers. When he stood to let her fling her legs out, Laney jumped out of bed and raced down the hall, not caring that she streaked past him.

Chanting, "No, no, no," Laney clenched her muscles to prevent an accident before collapsing to the toilet.

Returning at a slower pace, Laney found her bed remade with

Ballsy and Blueberry tucked in on her pillow. She leaned over the bed to press a good morning kiss on their faces and tried to stand up. Fane held her firmly against the mattress.

"I have a reminder for you to wear today," he explained as a rasp of something sounded softly.

"A reminder?" she echoed, looking back over her shoulder to see him setting a jar of lubricant next to her bottom.

"Yes. Now that you feel better, your task is to make everyone else happier, too. A plug in your bottom will help remind you to be kind today," he explained, taking a case from the nightstand and opening it next to her. Shiny metal anal plugs sparkled in the light.

"I don't want that in my bottom," she refused. Her muscles automatically contracted, drawing her buttocks close together.

"I know. Relax or this will be unpleasant," he counseled as his finger drifted over the array of plugs to select the correct size.

When he pulled the third one in the first row out, she protested, "The little one. It will be a great reminder."

Fane pointed to the first one. "You were unpleasant to me."

His fingers hovered over the second. "You were unpleasant to Arielle in the cafeteria."

Slowly, he ticked off enough people or places she had been short with until he reached the largest plug. Her eyes widened as she looked up at him.

"The third one is fine," she assured him.

"I'm glad you agree."

Laney watched him lubricate the plug thoroughly before handing it to her by the wide flange at the bottom. "What am I supposed to do with this?"

"Hold on to it while I prep your bottom."

In horror, she watched him scoop a dollop of lubricant on his index finger. As he moved it toward her buttocks, she felt his other hand slid down from her lower back to help separate her cheeks.

"No!" she wailed as he applied the cool mixture on her tightly closed opening. Despite her efforts to keep him out, Fane pressed the thick digit deep into her bottom and swirled the slippery gel to coat her tight passage.

She turned to look back at the plug and just barely kept herself from tossing it across the room. One glimpse at the others that waited in the case discouraged her from that impulsive response.

"Plug, please," Fane requested in a pleasant tone, as if he were asking her to pass the butter at breakfast.

Slowly, she handed it back to him as if it were a poisonous spider ready to bite her. "Daddy?" she tried one more time.

"You'll be a very good girl today. This reminder will help keep you focused," he answered.

Laney dropped her head to the mattress as the cold tip pressed against her puckered opening. Slowly, it stretched that clenched ring of muscles. At the widest, she rocked her hips, trying to make the burn stop.

"Almost there, Laney. Relax your bottom," he instructed.

"I don't want it," she wailed.

"I know. Cough," he said, surprising her.

"Cough?"

"Cough, Laney," he repeated, holding the thickness against her body firmly.

"Coff!" She pushed the air from her throat before rearing her head back as the invader pushed the last bit into her passageway and settled into place.

"There," Fane said with a tone of satisfaction.

"I don't have to wear this all day, do I?" she protested, wiggling her bottom as she tried to push it out.

"We'll see. One last thing to check." Fane removed a three-inch long device from the case and pushed a button.

Whirl! The plug in her bottom vibrated. Instant arousal filled her as the waves spread through her intimate spaces.

Laney looked at him, unable to believe what was happening. "You're not going to use that, are you?"

"Only when you need a reminder of the reminder," he said before clicking it off and dropping the controller in his pocket.

* * *

Laney moved awkwardly as she tried to ignore the object filling her bottom. It had warmed inside her now, so at least it didn't feel ice cold like it had in the beginning. At breakfast, Fane had shared that today was a day of atonement. Anytime she wasn't pleasant, no matter what the situation was, he would activate the vibration inside her.

Arriving in her office, Laney immediately headed for her private space. As she closed the door, a faint buzzing sound filled the air as her fingernails dug into the wood she suddenly needed to hold on to.

"Door open unless you have a private meeting," he instructed.

"I work better when it's closed," she invented, biting her lower lip to counteract the sensations coursing through her.

"Not today."

Carefully, Laney pushed the door back into a completely open position. Immediately, the device in her bottom silenced, and she sagged against the barrier for support for several seconds before pacing forward to stand by his desk.

Glaring at Fane, she hissed, "Give me that!"

"Nope. Go work. You've got a full schedule," he commented, pointing to the calendar on his computer.

"You are..." She struggled to come up with a good word to describe him.

"Elaine, thank you for meeting with me today," Belinda's friendly voice sounded from the doorway. Sensing something weird was happening, the tech expert asked, "Is this a good time?" as she looked back and forth between the businesswoman and her admin.

"Of course. Fane was just telling me who he had scheduled today. Come in. I wanted to talk to you about expansion plans," Elaine said smoothly as she indicated the way into her office.

"The buzz going through the building is electric after the board meeting," Belinda innocently shared as she preceded Elaine through the doorway.

A muffled choking laugh followed the duo, earning a glare from Elaine directed at the reception desk. A quick push of the button wiped that expression from Elaine's face as she realized Fane wouldn't hesitate to follow through if she didn't fit his description of a good girl. Plastering a smile on her face, she closed the door behind her.

One hour later, he tapped at the door before peeking inside. "Ms. Rivers, I'm sorry to interrupt you, but your next meeting is in ten minutes with Mr. Edgewater."

"Thank you, Fane." Elaine stood and rounded her desk to extend a hand to the other woman.

"I've enjoyed meeting with you. I have a lot of notes from items that we've discussed. Thank you for sharing your insight, Belinda."

"My pleasure. If you have any other questions, feel free to contact me."

"I'll walk with you down to the elevator," Elaine suggested. "What can you share with me about cyber security companies?"

"Oh, you don't want an outside company. They'll only give you part of their time and attention. You need someone full-time to be invested in Edgewater Industries. A permanent employee is best."

Elaine stopped in the hallway and fixed her attention fully on Belinda. "I can look at your file later, but while we're talking, I'll ask you directly. What specific training do you have in this field? Certifications or degrees?"

"I have a degree in computer science. I've taken a seminar on digital forensics. More important, I know the Edgewater Industries processes and systems. I'll be honest, Elaine, I'd like to be considered for this job."

"Noted. We'll create a profile of the skill set we need before considering staffing. The position will require specific knowledge and the ability to take charge of this area of Edgewater's tech system. I don't know whether another candidate will fit the job more precisely. I hope you'll be willing to work with someone else if you're not chosen," Elaine observed bluntly.

"I'm invested in Edgewater Industries, but I do wish to expand my work here to include new challenges," Belinda answered smoothly.

"I will share with you that Easton has plans for you. We are both impressed with your work here. I just don't know if this is the area he has in mind."

"Thank you for your honesty. I'll keep working to enlarge my skills and we'll talk when you're ready to make a move." Belinda nodded to Elaine as she stepped into the elevator, heading down.

Glancing at her watch, Elaine headed toward Easton's office. She had a lot to talk to him about. And she'd be out of Fane's view for a while. Being deliberately nice was exhausting.

CHAPTER 14

Walking into the cafeteria with Fane, Elaine pasted a smile on her face. A brief buzz made her clench her bottom as she turned to look at him. "What?"

"Don't look like you're going to your execution. Just be aware of the effect your laser focus on business has on others. Look, there's Cynthia from yoga."

"Hi, Cynthia!" he greeted her with a smile that sent a flare of jealousy through Elaine.

"Hi, Fane. Hi, Elaine. Sorry I missed class last week. I had a sick kid that infected my husband. He was a bigger baby than the two-year-old. Thank goodness, I love them both."

That resentful feeling inside Elaine withered as Fane confessed that he'd been absent, too.

"I hope they're both better now?" Elaine asked, surprised that she honestly wanted to hear they'd improved.

"Yes, ma'am. They were both on their feet in about twenty-four hours. Just long enough to equal three loads of laundry and a missed yoga class," Cynthia said with a laugh. "I'm off to help in the kitchen. Try the potato soup. I made it special today."

"Yum. Thanks, Cynthia," Fane answered as the busy employee dashed through the doors to the prep area.

"I may have soup today," Fane commented as he escorted her to the line to order.

"I don't know if I want something hot," Elaine confessed, scanning the list of daily specials. She liked to try different things.

When they reached the cashier, a very busy Arielle looked up to spot them. "Hi, Ms. Rivers. Hi, Fane. What would you like for lunch today? I promise to make sure they avoid mayo this time," she promised nervously. "I should have brought you a new sandwich. Mr. Alvarez was not happy with me. I promise I'll do better. I love my job here and need to keep it."

From the tone of her voice, Elaine could tell that Arielle was worried. The young woman's hands shook before she clasped them together at her waist. She looked back at Fane and met his knowing look. Mayonnaise wasn't worth the level of anxiety this employee was going through.

"I'm sorry, Arielle," she began before an older man hurried over to join them from behind the counter.

"Ah, Ms. Rivers. I was sorry to hear that Arielle screwed up your lunch order. It will not happen again. She has been warned and a letter placed in her file," the head of the cafeteria explained.

"Salvador, I want you to tear up that letter. It was an unfortunate misunderstanding that shouldn't endanger anyone's job. I believe that sandwich usually comes with mayonnaise?" Elaine paused for confirmation.

"Yes, ma'am," Arielle rushed to say.

"Then the blame rests solely on me for not asking for it to be changed," Elaine continued.

"That is kind of you to say, Ms. Rivers. But we in the cafeteria wish to support all our employees' preferences," Salvador Alvarez assured her.

"That is admirable. I prefer that my mistake not jeopardize someone's job. May I rely on you to remove that letter and erase any negative thoughts you have about Arielle's employment history?"

When the department head nodded his agreement, she continued, "I would like to discuss improvements and staffing needs, Salvador. Would you contact my assistant, Fane, when the lunch rush is over to set up a meeting?"

"Of course, Ms. Rivers." He jumped at the opportunity.

"And Salvador? Call me Elaine, please," she requested with a smile.

"I would be honored, Elaine." With a pleased look at Arielle, he excused himself when someone called his name.

"Now, Arielle. I understand there's a special potato soup Cynthia created today," Elaine ordered.

"She's the best cook. You're going to love it," Arielle rushed to assure her.

Elaine noted the employee risked a smile at her as if she didn't know what type of reaction she would get. "Now I know who to ask for recommendations. Thank you, Arielle."

They completed their order and moved to a table where it would be delivered soon. She looked at her assistant and shook her head. "Arielle confessed that my meal was wrong and received a negative letter in her file."

"You're important here. Very few of the employees know you personally. Easton, yes. You? You're the whip that keeps Edgewater Industries on course," Fane observed.

"And I've gone through a bunch of admins. They didn't lose their jobs, did they?"

"Fortunately, no. They jumped at the opportunity to get the raise offered by the position as your assistant. The increase in money is equal to the additional duties. I think they're all satisfied to make a bit less to have fewer responsibilities resting on their shoulders now," Fane answered.

"I don't mean to be a taskmaster," Elaine protested.

"You needed someone willing to work as hard as you do," he corrected her.

"Today has shown me that I need to work more on connecting with people. I don't want everyone to think I'm a tyrant."

She stopped talking as a server appeared with two steaming bowls of soup and a basket of rolls. After thanking him, she dipped her spoon in the soup and tasted it.

"Oh, yum!" she complimented.

"Cynthia's the best. The chef better watch his back. Anything she makes is top-notch," the server commented before leaving with a smile.

"This is good. I'm glad I ran into Cynthia," Fane commented, taking another bite.

When he waved, Elaine turned to follow his gaze. The server stood with the soup concoctor. Cynthia looked their way and smiled as Fane raised both thumbs up in approval. Not wanting to be left out, Elaine clapped silently and loved the cook's little bounce of happiness.

"You made her day," Fane observed.

"This really is delicious. She should get the recognition for her talent. Would you remind me to suggest to Salvador that he highlight different specials with a picture of the cook who created it? That way everyone could compliment them directly."

"I think that would be a great boost for morale and create a relationship between those nurturing Edgewater's employees and the staff. I know I'd be a grumpy guy if I didn't have such delicious food," Fane observed.

"Like you could be grumpy," she muttered before Fane's move to shift a hand into his pocket caught her attention.

"Wait! That was a good thing!" Elaine said quickly. "I wasn't being negative."

"Good girl," he praised in an intimate voice that only reached her ears.

* * *

As they walked outside at the end of the day, it dawned on Elaine that she hadn't felt his correction all afternoon. All day long, it had gotten easier to connect with others instead of focusing only on business.

"We got a lot done today," Fane mentioned.

"Almost everything on my schedule. That never happens," Elaine remarked with a laugh.

"You did well this afternoon. Everyone came out of your office with a smile—including you."

"I didn't want to get zapped," she whispered furiously.

"Hmm. Perhaps you need to wear a reminder frequently."

"No!" popped out of her mouth, drawing the attention of several employees walking nearby.

Automatically, Elaine smiled reassuringly at all as she expanded her statement in a voice they could all hear, "No, we haven't run into any roadblocks to the expansion plans."

Fane chuckled as he guided her down toward his car. After he shut the door, sealing them inside in privacy, she asked, "Will you take this out when we get home?"

A pleased expression slid over Fane's face, and he nodded before adding, "Only because you called it home, Laney."

Laney sat back against the seat and nodded. It was strange. She thought of his house as home already. *That must be a good sign.*

"What are we going to do tonight?" she asked.

"It's bath time when we get home. Then dinner. I thought we might play with the toys in your nursery or battle it out over a board game," he suggested as he drove into the garage.

"That sounds like fun," she murmured. Her body responded immediately to the idea of being naked while her Daddy bathed her. Laney squeezed her thighs together, trying to squelch her reaction.

"Stay there. Daddy will help you out," Fane reminded her as he turned off the engine.

Watching his athletic body, barely disguised by his office attire, Laney waited patiently for him to round the hood and open her door. Her fingers tangled in the narrow skirt of her usual business suit. As she stepped out of the car, Fane crowded her close to the vehicle. She could feel the proof of his desire pressed against her. When she looked up at him, he kissed her roughly.

"I always want you to think of where we are as home."

Fane captured her lips again to explore her mouth. When she

squirmed against him, trying to get closer, he stepped back when she gasped. "That plug is an effective reminder, isn't it?" He cupped her bottom with one hand and pulled her pelvis tight against him as it pushed the embedded device deeper inside her.

She froze in place, feeling her panties become soaked. Her Daddy held her effortlessly. He was in total control. Laney loved knowing that he was as aroused as she was. Never having dabbled in play back there, she was shocked at the desire that coursed through her. The metal flange tugged at her sensitive opening. Would he want to take her—there?

"Come on, Little girl. Let's get your cute bottom taken care of," he said, releasing her bottom to pat it softly.

"D... Daddy?" She stumbled over the word as he stepped away.

"Yes, Laney. Daddy will love you here soon. Your reminder to be a good girl can also stretch your tight bottom so I can make you feel good."

When she caught herself nodding without conscious thought, Laney's face heated and she knew her cheeks were bright red. She quickly looked down at the floor.

Fane caught her chin and lifted it firmly until their eyes met. "Between a Daddy and his Little, there are no secrets. I will explore you completely. Some things will drive you crazy with desire. Those will be your rewards. Others will force you past your comfort level. Those could be rewards or punishments."

As she pondered those words, Fane stepped back to take her hand and lead her through the garage. Halfway there, the light went out. Laney stopped immediately, trying to see through the darkness so she didn't trip.

"Trust Daddy," he requested as he brought her close. Fane turned so his back faced her. "Put your hands on my waist and we'll dance our way into the house." His hands closed over hers.

As he sang the silly song she'd first done as a child at the skating rink, Laney laughed out loud. Following the lyrics, she put one leg out to the side and then the other before hopping three times forward. The absolute darkness faded slightly as Laney's eyes adjusted to the gloom. Somehow, the blobs looming at her weren't so scary.

When he finally released Laney's hands to open the door, she was almost sad they couldn't play in the gloom anymore. With a final three hops, she landed in the interior of the house. The movement of the plug inside her was becoming urgent.

Reading her expression, Fane scooped Laney up and rushed to the master bathroom. He set her feet on the padded rug in front of one sink and pushed lightly on her back to lean her over.

"Brace yourself on the vanity. Keep your hands there, Little girl," he directed softly as he stroked down her back to her waistband. He left her for a few seconds to turn on the warm water in the tub. The crash of the water filled the air, seeming to create an even more private space around them.

Back at her side, he unfastened her skirt and let it drop to the floor. Lowering himself athletically to the rug, he pressed a kiss to the side of her thigh before helping her step out of the discarded garment as he stripped off her shoes. Fane scooped up her things and laid them on a handy bench.

"Panties next, Laney," he explained as he hooked his fingers into the elastic at her waist to coax the cotton and lace garment over her hips. Fane allowed them to drop around her ankles and left them there.

Being half-dressed made her feel more naked in front of him than if he'd undressed her totally. The air of the room wrapped around her bare flesh, making her shiver. The fabric looped around her feet kept her in place as firmly as shackles would have as he stroked over her bare bottom to cup her soft cheeks.

Unable to resist, Laney watched him in the mirror as he parted her bottom. His face reflected his desire—unguarded and fierce. Slowly, he pulled the plug from her bottom and placed it in the sink next to her. She stared at the reminder before looking up to meet his gaze in the reflection.

"You were a good girl today, Laney. Daddy's proud of you."

Triumphant pride filled her, making her push her shoulders back to straighten her spine. He stroked the back of his hand down her spine before swatting her bottom sharply.

When Laney jumped in reaction, he instructed, "Go potty and come back for Daddy to get you ready for the tub." Fane helped her step from her panties, leaving a kiss on the reddened spot on one cheek.

Freed from her position at the vanity, she fled to the privacy of the toilet area in the spacious bathroom. As Laney closed the door, she hesitated. Wanting to stay connected to him, she cracked the door to watch him turn on the water at the sink. Efficiently, he cleaned the plug and his hands before setting it to dry on a washcloth. The simple act assured her that, not only was he caring for her, Fane intended to use it again.

Without conscious thought, her fingers glided through the slick juices between her thighs. Tingles of bliss spread through her. Laney knew Fane would not approve of her pleasuring herself. He hadn't told her not to touch herself.

As if he could hear her thoughts, Fane spoke sharply. "Are you being good in there, Little girl?"

She snatched her hand away and quickly wiped herself dry before scurrying out to join him. Standing in front of him, Laney knew he was aware of her actions. She tried to meet his gaze without looking guilty, but couldn't. Studying her bare toes on the tile, Laney waited for him to punish her. When his hand lifted her chin until she looked directly into his eyes, she held her breath.

"Promise Daddy that your pleasure belongs to him."

"I… I promise." She stumbled over the words—not because she didn't want to agree, but because of the guilt Laney felt in doing something she knew he would not condone.

"Now you know," he said simply.

His words erased the worry inside her. Maybe she hadn't screwed this up. Tentatively, she smiled at him and nodded.

"Good girl."

Fane turned his attention to undressing her completely. When she stood in front of him nude, he gestured to the bathtub. "Get in, Laney. The warm water will ease the discomfort in your bottom."

Reminded of the invasion, she squeezed her cheeks together. "It's not bad," she whispered.

"I'm glad. Now in the tub. Daddy's going to let you soak for a while."

He helped her step into the warm water. It was perfect—not too hot or cold. With a sigh, she relaxed against the back slope and closed her eyes. Laney blinked up at the feel of his lips against her forehead.

"I'm going to start dinner. Don't fall asleep. I'll be back to wash you," he assured her.

"Okay, Daddy," she whispered and lifted her lips to invite a kiss.

He indulged her with a chuckle before standing. Fane turned down the brightness of the lights before he left the room.

Quiet serenity filled the beautiful space. Closing her eyes once again, Laney melted into the warm water. She'd learned so much since her Daddy came into her life about balancing work with enjoying life. Her stress level had diminished each day she spent with Fane as her assistant.

Sharon. She had found Piper for Easton and arranged for Fane to become her assistant. The woman seemed to have a knack for connecting the right people together. Laney knew Sharon's life was challenging now. Taking a moment to send her supportive thoughts, Laney hoped maybe it would help in some small way.

Feeling herself tense, Laney followed her Daddy's directions to unwind. She widened her legs slightly, allowing the warmth to soothe her bottom. Her opening didn't hurt—just reminded her of his control and possession. Exhaling completely, Laney savored the feeling of Fane wishing to take care of her so completely. She needed him in her life.

CHAPTER 15

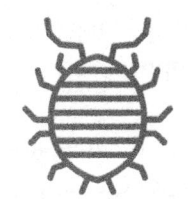

Laney snuggled against her Daddy. Sneaking a look at the clock, she knew their day would start soon and she wanted to treasure this quiet time with him. She'd slept so well after her bath. Fane had fed her and tucked her in bed early.

Now waking up refreshed and feeling loved, Laney compared her life just a short time ago with now. She'd been existing before, with a focus on achieving at a professionally high level. Since meeting Fane, business was still very important. It was just tempered with his insistence that she take care of herself as well. Laney really enjoyed having someone special focused on her.

I should do something special for him. Sneaking a peek at Fane's sleeping face, Laney decided to make him breakfast. They hadn't talked about her not using his kitchen.

Quietly, she rolled away from her Daddy's warmth, missing the contact with him immediately. Steeling herself from caving and curling back up next to him, Laney lowered her feet to the carpet and stood. Fane's regular breathing faltered slightly, and she froze in place. When he didn't wake up, she crept from the room and closed the door behind her.

Entering the kitchen, Laney took stock of the contents of the refrigerator. Eggs, orange juice, and a tube of biscuits. Her stomach growled. She pulled out her choices and set them on the counter next to a pile of mail that Fane had obviously brought in last night. With a flick of her wrist, she turned on the oven to preheat.

Laney slid the mail over slightly to make room for the small sheet pan. Several pieces dropped to the floor.

"Shoot!" she fake swore before laughing at herself. Laney had avoided curse words for so long to maintain the professional demeanor she thought was appropriate, she'd almost forgotten how to curse.

She leaned over to pick up the mail and set everything back on the counter. A pink envelope captured her gaze. Laney pulled it out of the stack and looked at it. The sender had written Fane Bogart and his address in a beautiful, flowing script. That had to be from a woman. A faint whiff of perfume drifted her way, making her lift the paper to her nose.

Instantly jealous, she looked for a return address. The upper corner was blank, but her fingers brushed over something raised on the back. Flipping over the letter, she stared at the old-fashioned red wax seal. *Daddy.*

Fane already had a Little girl. He'd lied to her. She had to get out of there. Laney was halfway out of the kitchen before she dashed back to turn off the oven. Even while totally pissed at him and heartbroken, she couldn't leave it on, possibly endangering his safety.

Rushing to the nursery, Elaine gathered her phone from the charger. Fane had added an outlet to a drawer to shut her phone away while she was in her Little space. Frantically, she pulled up a ride sharing app and requested a car. Someone was close. They'd be there in ten minutes.

Quickly, she searched for clothing to wear. Yanking off the soft nightshirt, she pulled on leggings and a T-shirt from the closet. Her bra and panties were in the master bedroom with her adult clothing for work. She couldn't go back in there. Rolling her eyes at her stupidity, Elaine realized her employee ID was in Fane's car where she'd tugged it off her blouse to drop the plastic card in the console's cupholder. The light switch was inside the garage. She wasn't going into that pitch dark area by herself. Now, not only would she have to take a walk of shame from the gate, she'd have to get a new ID card made.

Her gaze focused on the beautiful bed. Ballsy looked back at her in alarm. The well-loved stuffie always knew when she was upset. Thank goodness she hadn't left him there. He was snuggled up to Blueberry. Elaine snatched the soft bunny up as well. Tears filled her eyes for the first time. She needed something to remember her time with Fane.

Wrapping the two stuffies in another T-shirt, Elaine turned off the light in the nursery. She crept down the hall through the great room and attached kitchen. The groceries still standing on the counter reminded her of how much she'd lost in a few seconds. Would she have ever known that her Daddy was involved with another Little girl if she hadn't found that envelope?

Stiffening her back, she hurried to the door and let herself out silently. Hurt, so terribly hurt by his deception, Elaine checked her watch. Two minutes later, a compact car pulled into the driveway. Her professional mind still operated enough to compare the license plate with the app to ensure her safety. *Thank goodness for routines.*

***

"Good morning, Ms. Rivers. Do you need a ride to Tower B?" the guard at the gate to Edgewater Industries questioned when she exited the rideshare just outside the gate.

"Thank you, Jim. I'd appreciate that."

Elaine didn't want to imagine what the quiet security man thought as he drove her through the growing traffic of people reporting to work. Her phone had buzzed incessantly with incoming messages from Fane. She saw Jim glance at her device, but thankfully, he didn't ask any questions.

Walking through the glass doors, Elaine headed for the elevator. Catching a glimpse of Knox, she altered her course to run into him as he approached the front desk.

"Knox, I need to remove Fane from the approved guest list to my floor. I'll also need to deactivate my ID card and get another, please."

"I can do all that as soon as I get to my desk," he assured her. Concern beamed from his gaze. "I know something has happened. It's none of my business, but have you talked to Fane? Sometimes misunderstandings can be easily resolved."

"I agree. It is none of your business. Thank you for taking care of your job," she snapped, on the edge of losing control. Blinking furiously, Elaine clung to her dignity. She refused to cry in the lobby.

At Knox's nod, Elaine whirled back to the elevator and took shelter in the deserted car, away from anyone's eyes. She barely kept herself from running down the hall once she emerged from the elevator on her floor. Finally, she locked herself inside the apartment that felt funny now. It seemed abandoned and uninhabited. Bracing her shoulders against the wood door, Elaine finally allowed the tears to cascade down her cheeks.

Fane already has a Little. How can he do this to me?

Elaine allowed herself exactly five minutes to cry. She then wiped the moisture from her eyes and stiffened her spine. Stalking to her desk, she opened her personal computer and logged into the Edgewater Industries portal. She sent a message to Easton.

Please notify me when Fane Bogart's transfer to another position is complete. Until that time, I will work from home.

She was done with being manipulated. Elaine had dedicated several years to building Edgewater Industries. It would be hard to leave, but she'd have to if forced to work with Fane.

Her phone rang, and she looked at the caller ID by habit. Easton.

"Hello?"

"Elaine, we need to talk. Please come to my office at ten o'clock." Easton's voice was professional.

"I'll be there to meet with you alone," she stressed.

"Just you and I," Easton assured her.

Disconnecting, Elaine saw another message from Fane come across her screen. Unable to stop herself, she opened the window and read. The first messages were filled with concern for her safety. That had morphed to questions about what was going on. Finally, Fane asked to meet with her to clear up the confusion.

Please stop messaging me. I know what's going on and how you've lied. Clear your desk of your possessions immediately and await reassignment.

A new message buzzed in as she watched.

You've misunderstood...

She read only the first two words before pressing the button to block his number. Elaine was done.

Picking up the bundled T-shirt, Elaine walked into her bedroom and unwrapped the two stuffies. She kissed each one as she tucked the roly poly and the bunny under her covers. With a final pat on the comforter, she walked back into her closet and selected clothes for her meeting with Easton.

Her stomach gurgled from hunger as she emerged dressed in a severe black dress and pumps. Elaine smoothed down the skirt before heading into the bathroom to apply her makeup. Using the older containers she hadn't taken to Fane's home, she erased any sign of sadness and replaced it with her professional face. Edgewater's second-in-command was ready to go.

She took the elevator to the basement, wishing to avoid Knox at the front desk. Striding through the underground tunnel to A Tower, Elaine organized in her mind what she'd say to Easton. Their relationship had always been professional—she'd maintain her business persona.

Taking the elevator directly to Easton's office, Elaine headed for Piper's desk. "Good morning, Piper. I have a ten o'clock appointment with Easton. Is he ready for me?"

"Hi, Elaine." Piper leaned forward to whisper, "I'm sorry," before announcing, "Mr. Edgewater is free now if you'd like to go into his office."

Ignoring the private message, Elaine nodded and turned to enter her boss's office. Easton stood as she walked in and gestured to a chair in front of his desk. "I'm glad to see you, Elaine."

"We should have resolved this issue when I asked previously," she answered coldly. "Has Fane been removed from my office?"

"I think the two of you need to talk," Easton began, and paused when Elaine interrupted.

"I wish to focus on Edgewater Industries and nothing else," she stated firmly. "Has Fane been removed from my office?"

"Not yet. I would like the two of you to talk. I will be glad to arbitrate a meeting…"

"No, thank you. I will work from my apartment until you notify me he has vacated my office. Easton, I will be candid. I made a mistake in allowing Fane to enter my life. I've always kept my private and business lives separate. This is obviously the practice I need to return to."

When he spoke once again, she continued to talk over him. "Working remotely is not optimal. If I do not hear from you in three days, I will tender my resignation so that you can find a replacement who is able to work in that office."

"That is not necessary, Elaine. I'm simply asking you to speak to Fane. After that meeting, I will transfer him immediately if you wish."

"Easton, please put aside any attempts to rectify this matter. It simply is none of your business."

Her boss nodded. "I think you're making a mistake, but you're correct. This isn't officially Edgewater Industries' concern. The function of the company is my business. As one of my employees, I need you working at full power."

"I will do my best as soon as you free up my office for me to work there. In the meantime, I'll be at my apartment," Elaine answered. She knew he insinuated that her productivity had increased with Fane's planned interruptions in her work schedule. He was right. Catching that mistake in the surveyor's report had only happened with Fane's assistance.

She turned to leave and paused at the door. "Make sure he ends up in a good place." Walking quickly, Elaine distanced herself from his possible reply.

CHAPTER 16

One day later, Fane sent a message. *I am no longer your assistant. I will always be your Daddy. When you are able to talk, I'll be here.*

Somehow, Elaine's triumph didn't feel like a victory. She gathered up her materials from home and walked to A Building. Focused on her path, she did not acknowledge or even notice any of the greetings or calls of the employees she'd met during her time with Fane.

Exiting the elevator, she walked down the hall to her office. In the middle of the hall sat a desk with a familiar set of office toys scattered over the top. A colleague ran into her from behind when Elaine stopped abruptly.

"Whoops! You haven't seen Fane, our new hallway monitor, Ms. Rivers? He's a hoot," the woman commented as she navigated around his desk to continue down the hall.

Elaine paused next to Fane's desk when he held up a life-sized stop sign.

"You can't sit in the middle of the hallway, Fane!" she hissed in a low voice when he'd allowed the employee to continue down the hall.

"I've been removed from your office. There were no desks available in the administrative assistants' area on the second floor. I'm just here until another desk comes available," he explained with a smile.

Standing, he scooted his chair in to allow the hall traffic to move smoothly around him. "I've put myself on your calendar for a meeting this morning. Is it convenient for me to talk to you now?"

"No. Consider that appointment canceled. I do not wish to talk to you," Elaine answered. She turned on her heels and continued down the hall.

Damning Easton for the wide hallways he had incorporated in the ABC Towers, Elaine pasted a professional look on her face even as she fumed inside. She considered reporting it to the fire marshal as a hazard, but his sideways desk didn't even take up a third of the spacious pathway.

She walked into her office suite and tried to ignore the empty space that had been Fane's. Walking into her private office, she turned on her computer and began working. A meeting reminder popped up on her screen and she canceled it.

I am not meeting with him.

Elaine dove into work. She was on the second page of a report from a division detailing a problem at their site when a second meeting invite appeared in the corner of her screen. Again, she refused it.

After this happened repeatedly every ten minutes or so, she opened her calendar and blocked Fane from accessing her schedule. Elaine returned to work but found herself waiting for another interruption. She realized she hadn't absorbed anything in the last four pages of the report. Grabbing a piece of paper, Elaine forced herself to take notes to concentrate.

At noon, Cynthia appeared with a tray from the cafeteria. "Hi, Elaine. I have your lunch order. I'll have someone come pick up the tray and dishes in an hour if that's okay?"

Her first inclination was to send it back. Elaine stood and gestured to the small table at the side of her office. "Thank you, Cynthia. Just set it there. I'll come to the cafeteria from now on. You are all too busy to bring food to me. Ignore it if you get another message from me."

"Oh, no. We wouldn't do that. I love bringing trays to people. Always feel free to order food!" Cynthia rushed to reassure Elaine.

What else could Elaine say? "Thank you again."

"You're welcome. Enjoy!" Cynthia smiled at Elaine before leaving.

Knowing it was ridiculous to waste the delicious-smelling food out of spite, Elaine got up from her desk and ate there. The sandwich and salad were exactly what she would have ordered herself. There was no doubt who had ordered this. Fane was still taking care of her.

Elaine refused to let his kind gesture fool her. She repeated in her mind, "Fane has another Little. He lied." Each time, it seemed to lose a bit of the shock value she'd felt when she found that envelope.

After finishing her lunch, Elaine immersed herself in work. She tried to ignore her growing need to use the restroom. Determined not to go back into the hall until he'd left for the day, she tried to convince herself she didn't need to go.

"I'm leaving my desk to take a file to C Tower," flashed on her computer.

Elaine watched the clock and, after three minutes, dashed into the hall, past his empty desk, and into the bathroom. *No, no, no, no, no!* she chanted in her head as she slid the tight skirt up over her hips. *Made it!*

Hurrying back into her office, she found a sticky note on top of that pink envelope sitting on her keyboard. *Open it!*

Fane hadn't been at his computer when she'd returned, but somehow, he'd come in while she was in the restroom. Elaine inhaled. She could faintly smell his unique scent—warm, male, Fane. Her knees buckled, and she sat down in her chair. She was so screwed. Her heart and mind were in two completely different spaces.

Picking up that pink envelope, she opened the bottom drawer and dropped it inside. Elaine couldn't open it. Maybe another day. Not today.

* * *

By the third day, Elaine wanted nothing more than to work from home. Her head pounded with the stress of having him a short distance from her doorway. Fane continued to send periodic meeting requests from different emails. She blocked each one.

A knock on her door pulled her away from the project she had embroiled herself in. Looking up, she saw a man and woman at her door, each wearing a visitor tag.

"You must be in the wrong office. Who are you looking for?" she asked politely as she stood.

"Are you Elaine Rivers?" the young woman asked.

"I am. Did we have an appointment?" She moved to pull up her calendar, but the man's words stopped her.

"You haven't read the letter yet, have you?" His voice was filled with power—gentle, but with underlying steel.

Elaine answered without thinking. "I can't."

"Then let me tell you what it is," the woman blurted.

"My name is Anabel. I met Fane in college. He and I were in a math class together. Thomas was our professor," Anabel explained.

"Fane tried to explain everything to me, but I wasn't getting it. I've never been good at math, and I hate it. Fane approached Thomas to get help for me. Daddy took me under his wing and tutored me privately."

"Daddy?" Elaine echoed, trying to understand Anabel's words.

"He's my Daddy. We've been together for several years. Married for three," Anabel clarified.

"Tell her the rest, Little girl," Thomas directed. His tone was mild but unrefusable.

"I was stupid in the beginning. I dated a few guys while I was seeing Daddy. He put an end to that. He gave me a second chance, but I definitely wiped out his trust. We've rebuilt that over the years, but I never want him to feel... Well, like you do now."

"I don't think you have any idea how I feel," Elaine corrected her bluntly.

Anabel looked sick. "I never thought my letter would cause Fane to lose his chance at happiness."

"I don't understand why you're here," Elaine said coldly.

"Because I screwed up so badly in the past, I always share conversations or letters with Daddy. He puts his stamp on it before I send anything. Fane isn't my Daddy, Thomas is."

Elaine didn't know how to answer that. She looked back and forth between the two visitors.

"That letter I sent has a wax seal on it. That's Daddy's stamp," Anabel rushed to add.

Thomas reached into his pocket and pulled out a polished wooden handle with a metal flat end. "I do not require Anabel to share her communications with other men. She chooses to share them with me. This is the stamp I use to seal her letters."

He rotated the device to show Elaine the word chiseled into the shiny brass. The letters were reversed, but she could easily make out what they spelled. Daddy.

"Will you read the letter now?" Anabel asked.

Nodding, Elaine opened her bottom drawer and pulled out the pink envelope. Opening it, she pulled out a sheet of stationery with strawberries streaming down one side as decoration. Elaine unfolded the page and read:

Dearest Fane,

I had to write when Daddy told me you'd found your Little girl. My heart is bursting with joy. I hope you and Laney are happy for a billion years to come and that she adores you as much as you love her.

Your math-phobic friend,

Anabel

P.S. Come visit us soon. Daddy and I would love to meet Laney.

"I DID NOT MEAN to cause a problem between you and Fane. I just feel awful. We flew here as fast as we could to talk to you." Anabel's voice drifted away as if she didn't know what to say.

A sound from the doorway captured Elaine's attention. Fane stood one step outside her office. He looked ragged. She could tell he had run his fingers through his hair in exasperation, just like he had many times as he'd organized things in her office.

"You're not her Daddy?" Elaine asked, frozen by her desk.

"Never. Anabel and Thomas are close friends. I knew Anabel wasn't my Little girl when I was nineteen. That fact has never changed," he answered, walking toward her. "You are the one I've struggled to find."

Elaine took one step and then another before running forward to throw herself in his arms. "I'm so sorry."

"I want you to promise me you'll talk to me if you ever worry about us, Laney." Fane brushed his fingers through her hair to cup the back of her head.

"I promise. I've been so stupid."

"Not stupid. Hurt," he suggested. "It's torn me apart not to be able to help you—to ease the pain I know you've felt."

The door closed behind them, but neither Laney nor Fane turned to look. In the silence that followed, Fane drew her face toward his. His lips met hers in a whisper-soft kiss that touched her heart. She entwined her arms around his neck before pressing her lips against his urgently. Laney plastered herself against his chest, needing to eliminate all the space between them.

Passion flared between them as Fane's hands roamed over her back. She could feel his cock harden against her. Fane still wanted her. Regret for losing days they could have spent together crashed over her and tears escaped from her eyes to trail down her face.

"Laney, Little girl? Why are you crying?" he asked, leaning back in concern.

"I hurt you. I didn't even give you a chance to explain," she sobbed.

Fane leaned down to scoop an arm under her legs to pick her up in his arms. He carried her over to the office chair behind her desk and sat down with her cradled on his lap. "It was all a very unfortunate set of circumstances, made worse by us not being able to talk it out. That can't happen again. Can you commit to at least listening to me next time?"

"I'd like to, but what if I make another mistake? I was so sure, Fane, that you were playing me for a fool."

"I enjoy life, Laney, but I also know what's important. I want you to think back on all our serious conversations. Kites, stuffies, or jokes weren't involved. It was just you and I focused on each other."

She closed her eyes as she recalled their time together. Fane was right. Laney always pictured him as a fun-loving man who brought joy and laughter into her rigidly focused life. He was really so much more than that.

"Do you still want me? You know… as your Little girl?" she forced herself to ask, afraid of his answer.

"You are my Little girl. For better or for worse. My heart can't handle you not talking to me again, so I'm going to ask one more time. Will you commit to listening to me in the future?"

"No matter what's going on?" she asked, trying to envision a time when she wouldn't be able to keep that promise.

"Yes. Our relationship must be as important to you as your business reputation. You've worked hard to achieve all your successes. Will you put that same energy and focus into our relationship as well?"

"I'm good at what I do here. I don't think I'm a very good Little girl," she admitted.

"You're not secure being a Little girl. It's a risk for you."

Laney nodded. "It's scary and thrilling and new all at the same time."

"How do you feel when we're together, Laney?"

She exhaled slowly, gathering her courage. "Better than I've ever felt before." Laney straightened his collar, giving herself time to think. "I promise to listen to you."

"Thank you, Little girl." Fane pressed another soft kiss on her lips.

"Is that it? Do you forgive me?"

"Of course. And you will forgive yourself after your punishment."

"My punishment?" she repeated, feeling her eyes widen in shock at his words.

CHAPTER 17

"I have to carry it home?" Laney asked, biting her lip at the sight of the paddle in Fane's hand.

"Put it in your briefcase, Laney," he instructed before returning to his desk that once again filled the empty spot in the outer office.

She stared at the hard wooden implement. He'd had it in the box on his desk the first day he'd arrived. It scared her. Fane had spanked her before, but only with his hand. Laney swallowed hard before her boss's voice in the outer office made her scramble to hide it in her satchel.

"Hi, Easton! Yes, I escaped from the hall. Did you wish to speak to Elaine?" Fane asked nonchalantly.

"I'd like to speak to both of you, please, if this is convenient."

That simple request skyrocketed Elaine to her feet. She smoothed her skirt down over her hips as she headed for the door.

"Easton, of course I have time to speak with you." Elaine waved him into her office as she stepped back to clear the way. Fane followed the founder of Edgewater Industries into the room and closed the door for privacy.

She watched Easton walk over to the window and look out over the campus he had created. Elaine joined him as silence settled over the room. Was he going to fire her?

Finally, Easton turned to her. "Elaine, I count on you as my second-in-command for extremely difficult tasks and advice. During your time here, my confidence in your dedication and extreme efficiency has grown by leaps and bounds. Life, however, is not just focused on making money and expanding business. It's easy to stick with what you're an expert in and so difficult to risk everything on what you don't understand at all."

"Easton, are you firing me?" she asked, stiffening her spine.

He didn't acknowledge her question but continued to speak as if she hadn't interrupted. "I'm older than you. I have more acquisitions and tough choices under my belt. One thing I know is no one should try to navigate through life without someone who has their back. I can say with absolute confidence that when it comes to Edgewater Industries, you and I fill that need for each other."

He held his hand up when Elaine opened her mouth to chime in. "I'll ask for your indulgence in letting me speak."

When she nodded, he continued, "Work is only one part of your life. Living is the other. I put you in a challenging position this last month—more challenging than any report or business decision. Fane approached me and requested to be your administrative assistant."

Elaine looked over her shoulder to meet Fane's gaze as he lounged, seemingly unconcerned, with one shoulder against the wall. He nodded once, acknowledging that he had pursued becoming her assistant.

"I could have talked to you, but I knew you would think of your position and the demeanor you considered integral to being my chief operating officer before you'd weigh the importance of living your truth. So I threw you into the fire, knowing that if you survived it, you would emerge stronger and happier."

"You knew I was Little," she gasped. "How?"

"Daddies always know. To a person not drawn to this lifestyle, it is not apparent. To those with special insight, a Little stands out like an emergency beacon."

"No one else knew?"

"Very few. Knox, a few of the security detail, a couple of others who attended your second interview years ago when you joined Edgewater Industries. No one has gossiped or shared that information. They protect Littles staunchly as they would want theirs protected," he reassured her.

"What's most important is I want you to be both successful and happy here. I've been concerned in recent months that you were close to burning out. When Fane came to talk to me, I hoped that this would be your chance for happiness—for you personally, as well as for Edgewater industries."

"You took a colossal risk," she observed. "This office has not functioned well this week."

"It has not. That cannot continue," Easton said bluntly.

He cleared his throat before continuing, "After you acknowledged how well you worked together while completing that last quarterly report, Fane and I talked about being a Daddy in a work environment."

Elaine sat up rigidly straight at the thought of the two men discussing her.

"Never discussing our personal relationships, of course," Easton added quickly when he saw her bristle.

She turned to verify that statement with Fane. Elaine relaxed slightly when he shook his head and crossed his finger over his heart. He had her back in all things. How had she jeopardized their relationship without taking the time to listen to him?

Fane pushed away from the wall and approached the two executives. "Thank you, Easton, for giving us this chance. Only time will prove to you that we can support each other at work as well as in our private lives. I have no qualms about the future."

"Edgewater Industries has been the most important thing in my life until recently. It is now in second place, but I can assure you my work here will not suffer," Elaine stated carefully.

"That is all I ask." Easton headed to the door before pausing with his hand on the doorknob. "My congratulations to you both." With a big smile, he nodded once again and walked through the door.

Fane closed the door behind him and walked forward to wrap his arms around Laney. "That man never fails to surprise me."

"He's pretty incredible. He could have come in here and dropped the hammer on me. Edgewater Industries could operate like everyone else and only focus on the bottom line."

"He's a smart man. You're a big component in his company's achievements. Eventually, you would have left when you only had work to sustain you."

"That sounds like a fact you might have shared with him during your meeting."

"It was," Fane confirmed.

"Are we going to be okay?" she whispered.

"Nope. We're way past okay and heading toward stellar," he assured her.

"He's right. I was burning out," she admitted. "Easton's pretty much always right."

Laney looked at Fane. "That reminds me of someone else. How are we going to balance our private relationship and our personal one?"

"We're going to talk a lot and trust each other. You're the business expert."

"And you're the Daddy."

Fane tapped her bottom meaningfully. "I'm the Daddy, Little girl."

* * *

SIGHING, Laney set down her pencil before shaking out her hand. "I'm finished."

Fane put down his book and picked up the paper she'd hunched over for the last hour. Her sentences of *I will not refuse to talk to my Daddy in the future* filled the lines front and back. He nodded approvingly.

"Go get the paddle."

"Please. Can't this be my punishment?" she pleaded.

"How miserable were you?"

Laney dropped her gaze. He was right. Thinking he had a Little girl had devastated her. If she'd only let him explain.

Standing, she walked over to her briefcase and withdrew the thick wooden paddle. She stroked over the engraved letters on one side. This was going to hurt so bad. Maybe he'd take it easy on her.

"Bring it here, Little girl," he instructed softly.

"I don't want to," she wailed.

"I know."

Slowly, Laney walked toward her doom. She handed him the paddle and hesitated.

"This paddle is going to hang on the wall here in the kitchen to remind you to behave. I will not hesitate to use it in the future when you need it. But for now, go place it on the hook there," he directed, pointing to an empty space on the wall.

Eagerly, she almost skipped over to place it where he indicated. Turning around, she saw Fane had stood. His fingers unfastened the buckle at his waist before he pulled his leather belt from his pants.

"You're going to use your belt?" she whispered.

"Yes."

"Is it going to hurt?"

"Yes."

Her heart sank in her chest as she watched him curl the leather strip around one hand. Her gaze fixed on it as she froze in place.

"Come here."

Walking stiffly, she took baby steps toward Fane. When she stood in front of him, he sat down in his chair to guide her between his legs. After setting his belt on the table, Fane tugged her stretchy leggings and panties over her hips. Silently, he helped her lie over his lap.

Laney dangled helplessly over his hard thighs. Her fingertips and toes barely grazed the carpet. She jumped as his hand brushed over her bared bottom.

"Littles make bad choices sometimes. It's their Daddy's responsibility to help them make better choices in the future. Daddies also know that Littles are harder on themselves than anyone else is and that they need to have those mistakes wiped away. I'm spanking you today, not out of anger, but to help you move on and forgive yourself."

He rubbed her bottom as she considered his words. She hadn't been able to forgive herself for being too stubborn to let him explain. Now, looking back, it would have taken him two minutes to set everything straight. Instead, Anabel and Thomas had traveled across the country to explain.

"I'm ready, Daddy," she whispered, feeling tears streaming down her cheeks already. Laney shivered at the sound of the buckle jingling as he picked it back up.

"Count with me to ten, Laney," he instructed.

Whoosh! A strip of heat flared across her buttocks and she heard him announce, "One." Quickly, she echoed her Daddy. By the time she'd sobbed six, Laney squirmed over his lap. He'd captured her hands in his left one when she'd reached back instinctively to stop him.

"No more, Daddy. No more!"

"Four left. You can do this," he assured her before flicking the belt against her cheeks again.

The last three came with a flurry of sobs and thrashing. Laney collapsed over his lap as she repeated ten. She'd done it.

Without a word, Fane gathered her in his arms and lifted Laney to hold her against his chest. He supported her with her punished bottom extending off his thighs. "It's all over. You were very brave. Daddy's proud of you."

"I'm proud of me, too. That hurt," she admitted, reaching back to rub her buttocks.

His hand captured both of hers and restrained them at her waist. "No touching."

Fane rocked her slowly, wiping her face from time to time as he allowed her to recover. When Laney drew her head from the curve of his neck to peek up at him, he smiled gently at her.

"Feel better?"

"My heart does. My bottom may never forgive you," she admitted.

"I can live with that. I'm not above sweet talking your lower half." Fane waggled his eyebrows at her suggestively.

"Daddy!"

"Yes, Laney girl. I plan on being your Daddy until my last breath. Just make it a bit easier for me, huh? I lost a few years off my life when I thought I'd lost you."

"I love you."

"I love you, too, Little girl. Let's go put you in a cold bath to soothe your bottom."

"Thank you, Daddy." Laney knew he hadn't spanked her in anger. He'd corrected her behavior with love. The punishment had underlined how much he cared for her. If her Daddy wasn't committed to her, he wouldn't care if she remembered or not. Her bottom would not ever allow her to forget this lesson.

CHAPTER 18

Three months later, Laney carried the last of her clothing into her Daddy's house. She hadn't slept in her apartment since the day she and Fane had solved the pink envelope problem. Now, looking back, Laney could only shake her head at the anguish that she had gone through simply because she wouldn't listen to Fane.

Anabel and Thomas had become friends of hers as well. The two couples had spent a long weekend in each of their cities. It was obvious that Anabel and Thomas were dedicated to each other. She loved seeing the example of how a Daddy and Little girl could create a lasting relationship that supported them both.

"I think that's everything. Do you want to go back one more time to say goodbye to your apartment?" Fane asked, jingling his keys.

"No, Daddy. I think I said goodbye to Tower B a few months ago. I love living here with you," she confessed.

"And I love having you here. Come on, let's put your big girl clothes in the master closet."

"I'm tired, Daddy. Can we just relax tonight and watch a movie?"

"I think that's a perfect plan. Want to go pick out a movie and I'll get us something to drink?"

"Could I have chocolate milk?" Laney asked. She knew it would take her Daddy a few minutes to stir in the chocolate syrup.

"Of course."

Laney watched her Daddy walk to the kitchen. He looked as good going as coming. She hoped she'd always love to look at him.

When Fane turned and caught her ogling him, he winked and reminded her, "Movie, Little girl."

Scrambling, Laney grabbed the remote and opened their subscription streaming service to check out the movies. Choosing one with singing animals in a contest, she made sure it was ready to go and paused it to wait for her Daddy.

With that all set up, she called to the kitchen, "I'm going potty before the movie."

"Good idea! Call Daddy if you need help."

"Okay!" Laney dashed down the hall.

"No running," followed her.

Giggling, she dropped to her knees in front of the cabinet under the sink. Reaching past the towels stacked neatly, she found a can she had stashed there the last time her Daddy had been out of the house. It had been tricky to get it smuggled in without him seeing it. Now she was ready to show her Daddy that she knew how to have fun, too!

Quickly, she used the toilet and then waited inside the bathroom. Laney knew he'd come check on her.

"Little girl? Are you okay?" Fane's concerned voice drifted down the hallway.

"Daddy," she gasped, pretending that she could barely answer.

Immediately, heavy steps pounded down the hallway. The door flew open and Fane burst into the room. Immediately, Laney pressed the button on the top of the can she'd hidden in the bathroom. A stream of pink plastic spray flew out of the can's nozzle to attach itself to her Daddy.

"What?" he exclaimed as the stringy substance continued to target him.

"Oh, you're in big trouble, Little girl," he threatened. Fane's laughing eyes and grin erased any concern that she'd gone too far. Holding up his hands in front of his face as a shield, he walked forward, keeping his sight clear as Laney attempted to dodge around his barrier.

Pffft! Laney shook the can desperately. *It can't run out now!*

With one last burst of pink, the final bit of pressurized air exploded from the can. Laney dropped the can to the floor and tried to dart around her Daddy as he tried to extricate himself from the web of pink strings.

"Gotcha! Look how you've abused your Daddy," Fane laughed, catching her around her waist.

"It all comes off, Daddy," Laney promised as she pulled a few strands from his hair.

"You know we're going to have a shootout tomorrow when I arm myself."

"A shootout?" she questioned.

"Ten paces and then draw, partner," he drawled, tipping an imaginary cowboy hat.

Giggling, she nodded eagerly. "I'm taking you down, Daddy."

"Then I'm taking you up!" Fane leaned down to scoop Laney up on his shoulder, carrying her through the house.

"Daddy!" Laney laughed, holding on to his belt as she bounced on his shoulder.

"Laney!" he echoed before dropping her down to the sofa. Urgently, he yanked off his T-shirt before stretching out next to her. His hands swept over her body as she squirmed underneath him.

"I thought we were watching a movie?" she whispered between the kisses he delighted her with. Her fingers traced the bright new tattoo over his heart. Her name, written in beautiful script letters, permanently added to the intricate decorations on his skin. She leaned forward to kiss the *A* in Laney that suspiciously looked like a roly poly while the *Y* resembled bunny ears.

Framing her face with his hands, Fane growled, "Movie, later. Laney, now."

An image of her lonely apartment popped into her mind. It seemed like a lifetime ago that it had seemed like home. Her one-dimensional world had burst into color. As he stripped off her shirt, Laney basked in knowing that her Daddy was watching.

EPILOGUE

Sharon guided Roger to his usual chair on the deck. His faltering steps moved slower than it would have taken him to run a mile just months ago. She collapsed into her own chair and looked out over the lake view that had compelled their purchase of this house.

"Roger, do you remember when we first walked out here on the deck? I love this view as much today as I did then," Sharon commented.

"Don't be sad when I'm gone, honey. No one wants to live like this."

Sharon whirled around to meet his gaze. Roger's beautiful blue eyes looked back at her, clear of the fog that usually clouded them. His moments of lucidity came extremely rarely now.

"Daddy," she breathed. "Don't…"

"I love you, Sharon. Remember that. Forget all this. Live a magnificent life. I want…" His voice drifted off as he turned to look at the water.

"Daddy, what do you want?" Sharon held her breath, waiting for his answer.

Long seconds ticked by as she forced herself to be patient. Finally, she asked, "Can you look at me, sweetheart?"

When he didn't respond, Sharon stood and walked before him. Bracing her hands on the arms of his chair, she leaned close to him and froze. The sparkle of his eyes had vanished almost as if a light had been turned off behind them. Roger looked at her blankly before leaning slightly to the side to gaze into the distance.

He was gone. Her mesmerizing Daddy had disappeared.

Standing, she held back the tears until she fell back into her chair. Then, she allowed them to stream down her face, grieving for Roger and herself and cursing the relentless progression of the disease that robbed her of the Daddy who'd loved her with every fiber of his being.

Sharon pushed away her worries about the coming months. No one could save either one of them from the anguish of this dreadful disease. She'd honor the love she'd shared with her Daddy over the years and struggle to remember the best of times when he was gone. What would happen then, she couldn't imagine.

Sharon crossed her fingers, hoping for the best. That's all she could do now.

When her phone buzzed, she pulled it from her pocket to see Knox's name on the screen. Reading the message, she relaxed against the chair back.

Need anything? I'm at the store.

"Knox. He always saves the day," Sharon realized, feeling the heavy weight on her shoulders ease slightly.

Thank you for reading DADDY'S WATCHING! I hope you loved Fane and Elaine's story as much as I do! Don't miss the next romance brewing at the ABC Towers!

DADDY'S SAVING

Only a Daddy could save her from herself now…

After a lengthy sabbatical to be with her terminally ill husband, Sharon Ross is finally returning to Edgewater Industries. Broken by her loss, and weary from constant caregiving, she is relieved to be back with the only family she has left.

Knox Miller has loved Sharon from afar for years, and he can't stand by as grief and exhaustion consume the Little girl inside her. A special Daddy's tender love and care could rescue Sharon from her misery, and Knox intends to be the one she can count on for that relief.

One-click Daddy's Saving NOW!

Don't miss future sweet and steamy Daddy stories by Pepper North? Subscribe to my newsletter!

I'm excited to offer you a glimpse into Sharing Shelby, an International Bestselling novel introducing SANCTUM, a protected community for Littles and the Daddies who love them.

One-click Sharing Shelby now!

5.0 out of 5 stars
Sharing Shelby
Reviewed in the United States on August 24, 2020
This was a sweet story of MFM ménage and age play, as a little girl finds her forever daddies. It also introduces the secluded neighborhood of Sanctum, designed just for age play families. I'm looking forward to more in the series!

5.0 out of 5 stars
Awesome book!!
Reviewed in the United States on April 3, 2020
I so totally loved this book!! A very special connection between a Daddy and his Little girl is amazing!! I fell totally in love with the characters and their story!! Lots of hot steamy sexy times adds plenty of spice to this book!!

5.0 out of 5 stars

Love it
Reviewed in the United States on January 12, 2021
So excited that I found this author. I love Littles stories. Two daddies and one little girl makes this a wonderful story.

5.0 out of 5 stars
One of the best authors around love her books
Reviewed in the United Kingdom on August 17, 2018
I absolutely love all the books this author writes as she pulls u into hers books like you are living her stories and makes her characters come a live I would give her a thousand star ratings I highly recommended her to everyone I know.

Sharing Shelby - Chapter 1

SHELBY DANIELS TWIRLED AROUND in the dressing room, making the pretty blue dress float around her thighs. It was the same color as her big, blue eyes, which made them stand out even more in her heart-shaped face.

"Hi, Daddy," she practiced softly in the mirror, but sadness shadowed her eyes. She had dreamed since she could remember of meeting her Daddy, well, Daddies, because her dreams always featured two men, but they hadn't appeared in her life. Her family and friends were all encouraging her to date and find her Mr. Perfect. They said it wasn't right for such a beautiful woman to not go out on Friday and Saturday night to flirt. Did she expect to have Prince Charming ring her doorbell?

They couldn't understand that Shelby preferred her e-reader to fending off the groping hands of men who were so wrong for her. Reading and rereading the erotic romances she had found on the internet inspired her hope that she'd find the men who were right for her. She just needed to keep looking. She knew her Daddy was out there. Shelby crossed her fingers as she corrected herself: she knew her Daddies were out there.

Picturing them in her mind, she knew they were strong and forceful. The details of their height and hair color didn't matter to her. Her Daddies were looking for her, too. They needed to find their Little girl, the baby whom they would care for completely. She knew it would be embarrassing at times. Her face colored in the mirror at the thought of submitting to the intimate care they would lavish on her. Their requirements would push her boundaries, but she wouldn't be able to refuse them. They were her Daddies.

A cough in the next dressing room startled the slender brunette. She glanced at her watch with dismay. Quickly, she unzipped the dress and hung it carefully on the hanger. She couldn't leave it here. Crossing her fingers once again that no one would be at the register, Shelby rushed to redress and run from the dressing room with her precious find cradled in her arms. She was in luck: no one was checking out. She put the dress on her credit card and waited long enough for them to hang a plastic bag over the beautiful garment.

Dashing out of the store, she ran as fast as her sandals allowed back to her office building. Her boss had been out this morning. With luck, he'd have meetings all day. She opened the door to rush into the air conditioning. Looking down to make sure she wasn't crumpling her dress, Shelby walked straight into a hard, male body. She bounced back, stumbling on her heels. Just as she was about to fall backward, a strong hand wrapped around her elbow to steady her.

"Whoa! You were going too fast there, Little girl. Are you okay?" a low, masculine voice enveloped her.

Shelby looked up into a handsome chiseled face. Her eyes drifted down his expensive, custom-tailored suit that hugged his broad shoulders. A warm feeling started in her tummy and expanded into her body. She hadn't had this sensation before.

She paused as they looked at each other. In a flash, she remembered she was late and stammered her apologies as she ducked around his body that almost spanned the width of the doorway. "I'm so sorry, sir. I should watch where I am going," she called over her shoulder as she rushed into the warren of cubicles. That feeling in her tummy scared her. What was her body telling her?

"Wait! Are you alright?" his voice followed her into the building.

The proverbial thumbs-up was the only answer she took time to give him as she escaped from his view. Finding her home away from home, she stumbled into her cube. She hung her dress on the cube wall and flung herself into her chair as she dropped her purse on the desk. Her fingers flew over the keys to log back into her computer.

Taking a deep breath, she felt her shoulders drop from around her ears. She'd made it. Looking up at her screen, she saw the blue sticky note: *You're late. Thank you for volunteering to work on Saturday without pay.*

Her head drooped despondently. "So much for going to play in the park," she mumbled to herself.

"He came by about five minutes ago. He looked pretty smug. I read the note. I bet he was going to ask you to work this weekend for extra pay. You just saved his budget by coming in late," a snarky voice came from behind her.

"Hi, Veronica. It's okay. I didn't have anything to do this weekend."

"You didn't buy that dress, did you? It looks like something a six-year-old would like," Veronica observed as she examined her long red nails for nicks.

"Oh, you know me, Veronica. I have horrid taste in clothing," Shelby answered with a smile. She was determined not to let the catty woman know she was bothered by her incessant negative comments.

If she had to work on Saturday, at least Veronica wouldn't be there. Shelby typed a quick message to her boss that she'd mark her schedule to come in as he requested. She wanted him to know she hadn't been that late. Maybe he'd let her leave at noon.

She turned to the stack of papers and started working. Her boss had left additional work for her to complete as well when he'd visited her cubicle. Starting to feel a little depressed, Shelby turned to look at the beautiful dress. It was so wonderful. "Worth it!" Shelby whispered before diving in to complete as much of the paperwork as possible.

She locked the picture of the handsome man and the feel of his body against hers into a small box in her brain and threw away the key. He was way out of her league.

Want to read more? One-click Sharing Shelby now!

Dr. Richards' Littles®

A beloved age play series that features Littles who find their forever Daddies and Mommies. Dr. Richards guides and supports their efforts to keep their Littles happy and healthy.

Available on Amazon

Dr. Richards' Littles®
is a registered trademark of
With A Wink Publishing, LLC.
All rights reserved.

SANCTUM

Pepper North introduces you to an age play community that is isolated from the surrounding world. Here Littles can be Little, and Daddies can care for their Littles and keep them protected from the outside world.

Available on Amazon

Soldier Daddies

What private mission are these elite soldiers undertaking? They're all searching for their perfect Little girl.
Available on Amazon

The Keepers

This series from Pepper North is a twist on contemporary age play romances. Here are the stories of humans cared for by specially selected Keepers of an alien race. These are science fiction novels that age play readers will love!
Available on Amazon

The Magic of Twelve

The Magic of Twelve features the stories of twelve women transported on their 22nd birthday to a new life as the droblin (cherished Little one) of a Sorcerer of Bairn. These magic wielders have waited a long time to take complete care of their droblin's needs. They will protect their precious one to their last drop of magic from a growing menace. Each novel is a complete story.

Available on Amazon

Ever just gone for it? That's what *USA Today* Bestselling Author Pepper North did in 2017 when she posted a book for sale on Amazon without telling anyone. Thanks to her amazing fans, the support of the writing community, Mr. North, and a killer schedule, she has now written more than 80 books!

Enjoy contemporary, paranormal, dark, and erotic romances that are both sweet and steamy? Pepper will convert you into one of her loyal readers. What's coming in the future? A Daddypalooza!

Sign up for Pepper North's newsletter

Like Pepper North on Facebook

Join Pepper's Readers' Group for insider information and giveaways!

Follow Pepper everywhere!

Amazon Author Page
BookBub
FaceBook
GoodReads
Instagram
TikToc
Twitter
YouTube

Visit Pepper's website for a current checklist of books!

Made in the USA
Monee, IL
04 July 2024